THE 4 HORSES

-THE FIRST MOVIE SCRIPT of the TRILOGY SERIES-

Erens Ludik

Dedication

First of all, I want to thank Abba Father God and His Son, Jesus Christ, for His goodness to me. Also, thanks to the precious Holy Spirit, the constant Helper in my heart and thought processes.

Thirdly, I want to thank both my parents Hennie and Anita who taught me positive lessons in life. As my father had passed away in 1994, my mother's constant help through thick and thin was and is still outstanding. Also respect to my stepfather, John Hoskins, for his great wisdom and support over the years.

Fourthly, to my precious children Christian, Jessica and Christel. May you fulfil your destiny in God.

Lastly, to my 2 brothers, Jacques and Hein. I am happy to have two great brothers but I am also happy that I am the youngest. ☺

Acknowledgements

This is the first movie script out of the Trilogy series and it's important to acknowledge that without the Trinity of God all this would not be possible. All glory must go to the Father, The Son and the Holy Spirit, the Three in One!!!

As the idea unfolded and was put into writing, I have some important people to thank who played a pivotal role in helping me through my exciting journey writing the storyline.

First of all to my mother, Anita Ludik-Hoskins, who helped me with the correct grammar. She was always there along the road faithfully helping as the script developed.

Secondly, Dr Andrew McDonald. A very good friend with a great sense of humour. A lot of the funny scenes in the script has to do with his input. He was also instrumental in editing the script. A true friend!

Thirdly, Stella Heyns who helped polish this initial rough diamond of a script into an eternal shining bright diamond. Her talent speaks for itself and she played an extremely important role bringing class to the script. I will be forever grateful for that!

About Author

Erens Ludik, an entrepreneur with a wealth of business experience, has a passionate heart for God and His people. He is a great encourager who aims to help people find their true destiny on earth. He has written an Epic Trilogy about the End Times in a movie script format. It's full of romance, drama, action and unveiling the End with great accuracy.

Contact Erens Ludik

Website: https://erensludikmovies.com/

Email: info@erensludikmovies.com

The movie starts with Revelation 1:1-3

Blue Letters on the Screen and a loud voice reading it.

[1] The Revelation of Jesus Christ, which God gave Him to show His servants—things which must shortly take place. And He sent and signified it by His angel to His servant John, [2] who bore witness to the word of God, and to the testimony of Jesus Christ, to all things that he saw. [3] Blessed is he who reads and those who hear the words of this prophecy, and keep those things which are written in it; for the time is near.

It is the year AD 95 and the apostle John is kneeling down in a small obscure cave on the Greek Island of Patmos, and he is watching how Jesus opens the seals.

Revelation 6:1-8

[1] I watched as the Lamb opens the first of the seven seals. Then I heard one of the four living creatures say in a voice like thunder, "Come!" [2] I looked, and there before me was a white horse! Its rider held a bow, and he was given a crown, and he rode out as a conqueror bent on conquest.

[3] When the Lamb opened the second seal, I heard the second living creature say, "Come!" [4] Then another horse came out, a fiery red one. Its rider was given power to take peace from the earth and to make people kill each other. To him was given a large sword.

[5] When the Lamb opened the third seal, I heard the third living creature say, "Come!" I looked, and there before me was a black horse! Its rider was holding a pair of scales in his hand.

[6] Then I heard what sounded like a voice among the four living creatures, saying, "Two pounds of wheat for a day's wages and six

pounds of barley for a day's wages, and do not damage the oil and the wine!"

[7] When the Lamb opened the fourth seal, I heard the voice of the fourth living creature say, "Come!" [8] I looked, and there before me was a pale horse! Its rider was named Death, and Hades was following close behind him. They were given power over a fourth of the earth to kill by sword, famine and plague, and by the wild beasts of the earth.

Next Scene in New York

It's the year 2035

Jodhi and Helen are in New York. They are picked up at the Jane Hotel by a taxi driver called, Rich, who is hyper and talks a lot.

The Taxi has a lot of Denver Broncos souvenirs in it. The Club Mascot is a stallion. There are also a lot of tags of John Elway in the taxi. **A song plays in the taxi, "Who let the dogs out " by Baha Men.**

JODHI

So, I see you are a big bad Broncos fan.

TAXI DRIVER RICH

Sure, thing, buddy. You see that photo of John Elway over there. (*Rich is pointing to it.*) It's gold, man. He was in my cab one night, and he signed it for me. I mean, he is a god in Denver. You like the football, man?

JODHI

Yeah, for sure. Well, I remember his famous Drive against the Dog Pounder's in Cleveland? When was that again?

TAXI DRIVER RICH

It was 11 January 1987. I say it was the greatest NFL play ever. They ask who let the dogs out? Well, boy, we did.

(Jodhi and Helen are laughing.)

TAXI DRIVER RICH

So, you guys are going to La Guardia Airport?

JODHI

That's right.

TAXI DRIVER RICH

Man, but you know what? When you've seen one airport, you've seen them all. They are structural boring concrete jungles.

JODHI

Yeah, you are right.

TAXI DRIVER RICH

So, you haven't been to D.I.A then?

JODHI

No.

TAXI DRIVER RICH

Man, that airport is one mystical, magical mystery. You know it's a fact, it's a fact, you know, it's a crazy fact, but it's a fact. The mother of all airports.

JODHI

How do you mean?

TAXI DRIVER RICH

It's a central conspiracy, right. The home of Lucifer, aliens, the Illuminati, The New World Order. Talking…That's just for starters. The world's top secret power players operate out of a labyrinth of tunnels there. It's a fact, so it is, it's a well-known fact, so it is.

JODHI

Really?

TAXI DRIVER RICH

You know horses, yeah? Well, as you enter the airport, they've got a statue of a stallion there. It's a big mother, that's a fact. That's a well-known fact. It's 666 hands high, so it is, 666 hands high, I say. And you know the strangest thing?
It's called Blucifer, right, like Lucifer, it's a sign for sure. Blucifer has flaming red eyes, the Devil's eyes, I say for sure. The gateway not to the souls, but hell for souls. Think man, some kind of Devil worship is going on there, now that's a fact if I say so myself, it's a bloody fact.

JODHI

You like a fact to yourself, eh?

TAXI DRIVER RICH

Yeah, I got a file of facts, man. You know it's all in the Book of Revelation. The 4 horsemen, the dragon, the beast of the sea, the mark of the beast. The apocalypse is already starting. Man, it's a fact, I tell you, it's a super fact, so it is. You see that building over there? (*pointing to the UN building*), well, I am telling you that's the house of the beast. Devil's work, it's a fact, I tell you it's a fact.

All this one world religion, one world political superstructure, it's a counterfeit. It's false idolatry. Man, I'd turn that place into a bingo hall, a soup kitchen, anything but what it is now!

I tear it down with my bare hands, brick by brick, stone by stone. Did you know I am a son of toil, right? It's a fact; you ask anybody in these parts, they'll tell you!

JODHI

It seems you know a lot about the Book of Revelation.

TAXI DRIVER RICH

Yes, man, you see that black Ferrari? I bet you that guy bet on the black horse in the Book of Revelation. The Book of all Books. He doesn't know yet it's the wrong horse!

And I tell you also another thing, 9/11 was an inside job! The USA was hit right where its heart hurts. The trading house of the world. Now that's a fact. The gold was underneath The Twin Towers, not Fort Knox.

JODHI

So, you are a bit of a conspiracy theory kind of guy?

TAXI DRIVER RICH

Conspiracy theory, conspiracy theory, you say? Well, let me tell you, it's all facts. All a fact I say, you ask any of my mates, and they'll tell you what I am telling you; it's all facts. So, you want a conspiracy theory? Well, what do you make of this one, eh…? You know that Beatles guy, you know the one, the one that sounds like he is from Liverpool, oh yeah, I remember, Paul McCartney. Well, this is a fact, I tell you a pure fact he was killed in 1966 in a car crash, and he was replaced by an imposter, a double, a doppelganger and he's got away with it for over 50 years. The rest of the Beatles went along with the play; now that's a fact.

(They are arriving at the drop off at the airport door.)

JODHI

Well, thanks for a very interesting ride. I can assure you we never had a dull moment. *(Jodhi and Helen are laughing.)*

TAXI DRIVER RICH

Ok, you two, be safe. I can tell it will all end well for you two. I tell you, it's a fact…
(Jodhi and Helen takes their suitcases. The taxi leaves.)

(Jodhi and Helen have a conversation before they enter the airport doors. They are standing outside the airport terminal sliding doors. They instinctively stop and turn to face each other; they hold hands and gaze into each other's eyes.)

JODHI

Helen, I know it's only been 2 weeks since you shook my world upside down, but you know something?

HELEN

What?

JODHI

You are my heroine, my inevitable inspiration. Helen, Helen, it truly is you who has opened my closed heart and my jaded mind.

The joy of songs is the key to love. Helen, I need to know something, something here and now.

HELEN

My dearest Jodhi, you can ask me anything, anything that is of this world, and I will move mountains to answer truthfully as truth is love, and love is truth.

JODHI

Helen, these airport doors are like the pillars of King Solomon, Boaz and Jachin. They represent the signposts for the final battle between good and evil. Once we cross this Rubicon, you know there is no turning back. You are my reversal of misfortune in life. I need to know if you will come with me to the far corners of the known world. You know what I am talking about, right?

HELEN

Solomon, eh? You well know that he could have had any gift he wanted from God, and what did he choose? He chose the gift of eternal wisdom. The rarest of gifts Mr Livingstone and so I choose you.

(Jodhi and Helen kiss.)

JODHI

Are you ready for Rome?

HELEN

Yeah, the Eternal City on earth awaits us.

*(**Song plays "Whenever, Wherever by Shakira**. Jodhi and Helen go into the airport.)*

(Flashback. Thirteen days earlier and events that led up to Jodhi and Helen's departure to Rome.)

(Jodhi has resigned from being a pastor at the Church because of Church politics. He had a few arguments with his staff members at the Church in Carmel on the Sea.)

Next Scene

(A scene where he storms out of the Church meeting with his staff. He is disgruntled, angry, and mumbling to himself. He phones his best friend Mikey because his wife does not talk to him anymore. The phone is ringing, and Mikey picks up the phone.)

MIKEY

Hey Jodhi, how's my best friend doing?

JODHI

Let's say I have seen better days, Mikey.

MIKEY

What happened? You don't sound like your normal happy go lucky?

JODHI

I have just resigned.

MIKEY

Gosh. Why?

JODHI

Let's say they are more old school than me. It's all church politics.

MIKEY

Well, that's not a surprise to me as you are too upbeat for them.

JODHI

Yeah, I need to go home now.

MIKEY

How's things at home with Emily?

JODHI

You know the story. We haven't been speaking for a long time. I think that's also up in the air. What can I say? I am living a bit of a nightmare at the moment?

MIKEY

Well, Jodhi, you know I'm always there for you. If you need to talk…Phone me any time.

JODHI

Thank you, Mikey. I better go now. Speak to you soon.

MIKEY

Cheers Jodhi.

(Jodhi is driving home. He arrives at his home. He goes to his front door. Emily opens the door and throws out a couple of his suitcases.)

EMILY

It's over. Finished. I want a divorce. Here are the papers. Make sure you sign them. I won't keep the kids away from you, but please just sign the papers! I am DONE!!

(Emily slams the door in his face. Jodhi picks up the suitcases and the divorce papers.)

Next Scene

He drives off to The Mission Ranch Restaurant at Carmel on the Sea, California. It's a farmhouse restored by Clint Eastwood. There are horses outside. He walks into the Restaurant.

A Robot dressed like Clint Eastwood greets him. "Welcome to Clint Eastwood Mission Ranch. Do you feel Lucky today, Punk?" The Robot pulls his gun out and shoots.

The Robot says, "Go ahead, make my day. **A song plays "Get Ready" by Blake & Pitbull.** *The waitress is dressed as a cowgirl. She welcomes him and takes him to his table.)*

WAITRESS KATE

Welcome, Sir. My name is Kate. Table for one, I assume?

JODHI

Yes, just me.

(Jodhi realises he is all alone. The reality hits him when he says that it is just him.)

(Kate takes Jodhi to his table and shows him the menu.)

WAITRESS KATE

Here's the menu. What do you feel like today? Maybe I can recommend something.

JODHI

I would like a steak and maybe a starter.

WAITRESS KATE

How about the Sergio Leonie soup followed by The Pale Rider steak?

JODHI

That sounds great! Can I have a peppercorn sauce for the steak?

WAITRESS KATE

Of course, and how do you want your steak done?

JODHI

Medium to rare, please.

WAITRESS KATE

Sure. Something to drink?

JODHI

Just a large Coke, please.

WAITRESS KATE

Coming right up, Sir!
(A guy called Cash is sitting next to his table on his own.)

CASH

I could not help overhearing - excellent choice! You won't be disappointed.

JODHI

Ok, then I am glad I took her advice.

CASH

My name is Cash. Pleased to meet you.

(They shake hands.)

JODHI

Don't tell me Johnny Cash. *(They both are laughing.)* Nice to meet you!
I am Jodhi. So, Cash, what are you doing around here?

CASH

I work on the tables at the Marina Club Casino.

JODHI

I see. I should have guessed that, with a name like that. *(They both are smiling.)*

CASH

Yeah, well... Cash is unfortunately NOT king anymore. Nowadays, everything is so digital. Computerised. On our phones, you know. I mean, they are even talking about using a microchip in your body to buy or sell.

JODHI

Yes, I know. We are truly living in the end times, my friend.

CASH

What do you do, Jodhi?

JODHI

Well, that's an interesting question. How do I answer that? I have just resigned as a pastor of a church and also just got divorced. A lot of life in one day, I guess.

CASH

Wow. Sorry to hear that, man. Sounds like you need a break!

JODHI

Yeah, I am doing that right now. I am just thinking what to do next.

CASH

Why don't you go to Vegas for a few days? It might bring you good luck.

JODHI

That's not a bad idea. I have never been there.

CASH

You should definitely go.

JODHI

You know what I think, that's exactly what I should do. Thanks for the idea.

CASH

You are welcome. I hope you have a better run of luck than Bugsy Seagull and Jimmy Hoffa.

JODHI

Thanks! (*Jodhi is smiling.*)

(*Jodhi's food and drink arrive.*)

WAITRESS KATE

Enjoy your food!

JODHI

Thank you very much!

CASH

I am on my way now. Enjoy your trip. I know you will have fun in Vegas!

JODHI

Thank you, Cash. All the best.

(*The two shake hands. Jodhi is eating his meal. Once he finishes, the waitress Kate, comes to his table.*)

WAITRESS KATE

I hope you enjoyed your dinner.

JODHI

It was first class. Thank you very much!

(Jodhi is making a payment with his phone.)

WAITRESS KATE

Thank you, Sir. Hope to see you again soon.

JODHI

Thank you, Kate.

(Jodhi is leaving the restaurant.)

Next Scene

*(Jodhi drives to San Francisco Airport. **The song plays on the radio, "Mr Brightside" by The Killers.** He arrives at the airport and parks his car. He goes into the airport with his suitcases and books a ticket to Las Vegas.)*

JODHI

When is the next flight to Las Vegas?

TICKET DESK ATTENDANT - a girl, called Destiny

It's in 2 hours' time, Sir.

JODHI

Can you please book me a return ticket? Returning on Wednesday, please.

DESTINY

Sure Sir.

(Jodhi receives the ticket.)

JODHI

Many thanks, Destiny.

(Jodhi walks off.)

(Jodhi is in Las Vegas. He takes a taxi from the airport to The Money Towers hotel.) **(Song plays in taxi "Viva Las Vegas" by Elvis Presley.)**

JODHI

Good morning. Can I have a taxi to The Money Towers hotel?

TAXI DRIVER

Sure thing.

(Jodhi is getting into the taxi.)

TAXI DRIVER

So, what's the crack? You all on your own here in Vegas?

JODHI

(Jodhi is laughing).

Well yeah, I feel I need a real break and let my hair down a bit.

TAXI DRIVER

Well, you are in the right place for that.

(Taxi driver is laughing.)

JODHI

I hope so. (*Jodhi is smiling.*)

*(The taxi is arriving at The Money Towers hotel. Jodhi is paying the taxi driver by phone. **Song plays "Money Towers" by Lydmor**.)*

JODHI

Thanks.

TAXI DRIVER

You are very welcome. Enjoy your time!

Next Scene

(Jodhi goes into the hotel. He books in at reception. Roxy works at reception.)

ROXY

Good morning Sir. How are you doing?

JODHI

I am fine, thanks. It sounds like you are from South Africa.

ROXY

Yes, that's right. How did you know?

JODHI

Because I am half South African. I was born there. I moved to the US when I was still in school.

ROXY

That is great! I am originally from Cape Town.

JODHI

Me too! "Baie goed om te ontmoet."
(Subtitles: "It's very nice to meet.")

ROXY

Oh, you haven't lost your Afrikaans? (*Roxy is laughing.)*

JODHI

"Nooit."
(*Subtitles*: "Never")

ROXI

"Baie goed."
(*Subtitles*: "Very good")

JODHI

It's nice to speak Afrikaans with someone who can understand the language.

ROXY

Yes, it is. It reminds me of home. There's no place like home.
(*Roxy smiles.*)

JODHI

So how did you end up here? (*Jodhi is laughing.*)

ROXY

I came with my father to a sports conference. We were promoting rugby in the USA. I decided to stay on.

JODHI

That's great. I played rugby myself at school in South Africa. So, who is your father?

ROXY

My father is Rob Louw.

JODHI

Wow, I always liked him. I think he was one of the best Springbok flanks ever. I will never forget the try he scored in Newlands, Cape Town, on the 1980 Lion's tour in South Africa.

ROXY

Oh, thanks.

JODHI

Have you seen the Clint Eastwood movie Invictus?

ROXY

Yeah, it's a brilliant movie!

JODHI

I can talk all day long about rugby, but I guess I should book my room. (*Jodhi is smiling.*)

ROXY

So how many nights do you want to stay with us?

JODHI

I was thinking 2 nights.

24

ROXY

Ok, no problem. What is your surname?

JODHI

Mr Livingstone.

ROXY

We have an available room on the 8th floor. Your room is number 888. You can take the escalator on your right to floor 8.

(Jodhi takes the keys and says goodbye.)

JODHI

I like that number. Maybe it can bring me luck.

ROXY

I hope so, Sir. *(Roxy is smiling).*

JODHI

Ok, thanks, Roxy.

(Jodhi goes to his room. Takes a shower. Puts the TV on. News flashes of economic collapses and the dollar are very weak. Jodhi gets dressed and gets ready for the night out.)

Next Scene

*(Jodhi enters the Casino at The Money Towers. **The song is playing "Toxic" by Britney Spears**. He gets a glass of wine at the bar. He orders a white wine. A blonde girl comes and sits next to him. They start talking.)*

SAUVIGNON BLANC

Good evening handsome.

JODHI

Good evening.

SAUVIGNON BLANC

You look as if you are new here. How long have you been here?

JODHI

I have just arrived.

SAUVIGNON BLANC

That's cool. You are going to have a lot of fun here. That's for sure. What's your name?

JODHI

I am Jodhi and you?

SAUVIGNON BLANC

I am Sauvignon Blanc. Nice to meet you.

JODHI

Nice to meet you Sauvignon Blanc. Is that your Vegas name?
(*Jodhi is smiling.*)

SAUVIGNON BLANC

Yeah, baby.

JODHI

So, what do you do?

SAUVIGNON BLANC

I am a minimalist wardrobe operative.

JODHI

What do you mean?

SAUVIGNON BLANC

In the old money, that makes me a stripper honey.

JODHI

Wow. I got it now.

SAUVIGNON BLANC

I work at the Paradise Gentlemen's Club.

JODHI

Ok.

SAUVIGNON BLANC

And what does Jodhi-honey do for a living?

JODHI

I was a pastor for many years but resigned this morning.

SAUVIGNON BLANC

Well, look at you – quite the operator! From pulpit to Paradise in one day... I like your style. (*She is smiling.*)

JODHI

(*Jodhi is laughing.*) Well, I guess it sounds very strange, but that's what has happened.

SAUVIGNON BLANC

No issues. Enjoy yourself. It's your life, and you are free to do what you feel you want to do.

JODHI

I will surely make the best out of my time here.

SAUVIGNON BLANC

Honey, I have to go now. Come around to The Paradise sometime and see me in action.

JODHI

(*Jodhi is smiling again.*) Nice to meet you.

SAUVIGNON BLANC

(*She kisses him on the cheek.*) Bye-bye Love! Don't be a good boy, now!

JODHI

Bye-bye.

Next Scene

(Jodhi is walking to the Casino tables. He sits at one of the tables. A Chinese girl called Candy joins him at the table. **The song plays "I Want Candy", sung by Charli XCX.***)*

CANDY

How are you doing? My name is Candy, and yours?

JODHI

I am Jodhi. Nice to meet you.

CANDY

Nice to meet you, Jodhi. Are you playing?

JODHI

No, just checking it out.

CANDY

Nice. What are you doing in Las Vegas?

JODHI

I am just here to take a break.

CANDY

I can show you the ropes. I am on the tables often.

JODHI

Like rope a dope. (*Both are laughing.*)

CANDY

Let's hit the tables before the tables hit us.

JODHI

Sure. So how long have you been in Vegas?

CANDY

For a while. I am originally from Hong Kong.

JODHI

That's interesting. I have never been there, but I know it's a financial hub in the far east.

CANDY

It sure is, baby.

JODHI

It's for a reason that China is the strongest economic power in the world.

CANDY

Yeah, baby, we are. Shall we play some Roulette? I am good at that.

JODHI

Sure. I haven't really played it before.

CANDY

Ok, I will help you. Do you know that the numbers on the Roulette table are adding up to 666?

JODHI

I didn't know that, but now I do.

CANDY

We can play the next game if you want.

JODHI

(Song plays "24K Magic" by Bruno Mars.)

Ok, I will probably need your help. Let's do it.

JAMES (on the roulette table)

Ok, you guys want to play?

JODHI

Yeah.

CANDY

(Candy is looking at Jodhi.)

If you put it on black or red, you can double your money.

JODHI

Ok, let's put a $1000 on red.

JAMES

(James is spinning the roulette wheel.)

Ok, guys, here we go.

CANDY

(The chip lands on red.)

Well done!

JODHI

Wow!

CANDY

(Candy gives him a high 5.)

That's brilliant. Now, if you put it on a number red or black, you can win 35 times your money.

JODHI

Ok, let's go for it. Put the $2000 on the number 8 red.

JAMES

(James is spinning the roulette wheel again.)

Sure Sir.

CANDY

(The chip lands on number 8 red.)

Incredible!

(Candy is hugging Jodhi.)

JODHI

(Jodhi is totally amazed and smiles.)

What can I say? You must bring me lady luck. You choose the bet this time!

CANDY

Ok, why don't you put the $70k on with another $23k? You can win $3.29 Million and give me some kickback. Candy do as Candy does. *(Candy is smiling.)*

JODHI

Why not? Which number and colour should I put it on?

CANDY

Put it on number 19, black.

JODHI

Ok, James, number 19 black it is.

JAMES

(James is spinning the roulette wheel again.)

Ok, Sir. Good luck.

(The chip falls on the number 3 black.)

JODHI

(Jodhi is shaking his head. He has lost in total $24k.)

That's me done.

CANDY

Sorry, Honey! Aaaaauw, let's go party your troubles away!
You can have some Candy for half price if you know what I mean.
Candy always makes it better... *(She is smiling.)*

JODHI

I would do anything for love, but I won't do that. *(Jodhi is smiling.)*

CANDY

Like Meatloaf. *(She is smiling.)*

JODHI

Bye Candy.

CANDY

Bye Jodhi, have fun.

(Jodhi goes to his hotel room. Jodhi gets ready for bed. He falls asleep. He starts having a dream about the 4 horses in Chapter 6 of the Book of Revelation. He sees 4 horsemen visually running over the earth. He wakes up and ponders about the 4 horsemen. He orders breakfast in his room. A robot is bringing it. He has orange juice, tea, scrambled eggs, and salmon.)

(It's a bright blue-sky day. Jodhi is looking up on the internet to see what shows are on in town. He buys an online ticket to watch Dua Lipa at The Cosmopolitan of Las Vegas. He showers and gets dressed. He is having a walk around the strip in Las Vegas.)

Next Scene

(He goes to the pool deck at the Venetian hotel. He goes to the men's changing room to put on his swimming trunks. He orders a drink at the bar and lies down on a sun lounger next to the pool. There is a girl next to him. They start chatting.)

(Song plays in the background "It's a beautiful day " by U2.)

JODHI

What a beautiful day today.

JASMINE

Yes, it is for sure. What's your name?

JODHI

I am Jodhi. Nice to meet you. And yours?

JASMINE

I am Jasmine. The pleasure is mine.

JODHI

You have a Scottish Accent.

JASMINE

Yes, I am from Glasgow, Scotland. The land of the great, good and black gold.

JODHI

I hear it's beautiful. I am half- Scottish, but I have never been to Scotland. The closest I've come is watching Braveheart. I mean - the landscape, the people, William Wallace – just epic.

JASMINE

Yeah, it is a great movie.

JODHI

Are you on holiday here?

JASMINE

Yes, I came with my friend. She is in the casino now.

JODHI

Well, I wish her luck. Luck was definitely NOT my lady last night! Seems like the story of my life at the moment (*pensive sigh*)

JASMINE

That's what happens in Vegas, but I bet you were born a winner. (*Jasmine is laughing.*)

JODHI

I believe so. (*Jodhi is smiling.*)

JASMINE

So, what are your plans for today?

JODHI

I have booked a ticket for tonight's show in the Cosmopolitan hotel. Dua Lipa is performing. She is so cool she could freeze the whole of Africa.

JASMINE

Oh wow, you'll enjoy it! I saw her show in Glasgow. She is so talented. A real class act. She was cooler than snow. (*They both are laughing.*)

JODHI

Yeah, I am looking forward to it.

JASMINE

You should go for a swim. The water is nice. (*adjusting her bikini top to show off her assets*)

JODHI

Yeah, I am going to do that now. I definitely need a cooldown.

JASMINE

Enjoy! You put the cool in the cooler. (*Jodhi is smiling. He goes for a swim and gets back to his sun lounger.*)

JODHI

Wow, that was refreshing.

JASMINE

I have something that is even more refreshing.

JODHI

What is that?

(Jasmine shows him a small packet of cocaine.)

JASMINE

Shall we have a few lines for – let's call it, new time's sake?

JODHI

I don't cross those lines, but thank you.

JASMINE

(Pouting.) Not even for the sake of Auld Lang Syne?

JODHI

Not even for a cup O'kindness for days of Auld Lang Syne?

JASMINE

Cool. *(Shrugs)* Your loss. More for me!

JODHI

Nice meeting you. I have to go now and get ready for the show. Enjoy the rest of your day!

JASMINE

Thanks. Enjoy your show!

JODHI

Thanks! Bye. Be lucky, lady blah blah blah. *(Both are laughing.)*

JASMINE

Bye, Mr Cool Dude.

(Jodhi goes to the men's changing room to get dressed. He walks back to his hotel and gets ready for the night.)

*(He walks along the strip to the Cosmopolitan hotel to watch the Dua Lipa show. He gets his ticket at the venue. **Dua Lipa is singing "Genesis".**)*

Next Scene

Late night,
Post-Dua Lipa show

(He is in his hotel room. He is watching TV. He sees a programme of people in the world experimenting to take a microchip into their hands and into their forehead. He watches in awe. He falls asleep. He dreams again.)

(He dreams about a time when all people are forced to take a microchip in their hand and forehead to buy and sell things. Also, people can't buy with cash anymore. He wakes up in a start and ponders over it. He goes to sleep again.)

Next Scene

(It's Wednesday morning, and Jodhi is leaving the hotel. He is saying goodbye to Roxy at Reception. A taxi is picking him up.)

JODHI

Good Morning Roxy.

ROXY

Good morning Mr Livingstone. I hope your stay with us was great.

JODHI

Yes, it was *(Pause)* interesting... Let's hope that what happened in Vegas really STAYS in Vegas! *(Jodhi is Smiling.)*

ROXY

(Chuckle)
I am glad to hear. Vegas has a way of being... interesting.
(Smiles mischievously)

JODHI

Totsiens!
(Subtitles: "Goodbye!"*)*
Maybe I'll see you in Cape Town one day.

ROXY

That would be awesome.

JODHI

My taxi has arrived. Thank you for the stay.

ROXY

You are welcome, Mr Livingstone. Hope to see you again.

JODHI

Bye-bye Roxy. I'll see you if you get there.

ROXY

Bye, Mr Livingstone. Enjoy life.

Next Scene

(The taxi is picking him up. He flies to San Francisco. He walks out of the airport. He gets a taxi to St Francis Hotel.)

TAXI DRIVER

Where are you going, Sir?

JODHI

Can you please take me to the St. Francis Hotel?

TAXI DRIVER

Sure Sir.

(Jodhi arrives at St. Francis Hotel. He says goodbye to the taxi driver.)

JODHI

Cheers.

TAXI DRIVER

Have a good stay, Sir.

JODHI

Thanks.

Next Scene

(Jodhi walks into the hotel and is greeted by Ruth at Reception.)

RECEPTION GIRL RUTH

Good morning Sir. How can I help you?

JODHI

Good morning Ruth. Can you please book me a room for 7 days?

RUTH

Sure Sir. Your room number is 18. It's on the 3rd floor.

(Ruth gives him the keys.)

Next Scene

(Jodhi is in his room. He gets on google on his phone and looks for any managerial jobs in San Francisco. He sees a managerial position advertised at Carnegie Scrap Metal Dealers. He phones the yard.)

JODHI

Good morning. Could I please speak to the owner?

RECEPTIONIST ANITA

He's kind of busy all day, sir. What do you want to speak to him about?

JODHI

My name is Jodhi Livingstone. It's about the job advertised online.

RECEPTIONIST ANITA

Ok, please hold on, Mr Livingstone. I will see what I can do.

(The Receptionist speaking to Mr McDonald and put Jodhi through on the line.)

MR MCDONALD

Good day Mr Livingstone. It's Mr McDonald here.

JODHI

Good day Mr McDonald.

MR MCDONALD

My receptionist is telling me that you are interested in the managerial position that's available.

JODHI

That's right, I am very interested.

MR MCDONALD

Ok. Have you got any experience in the metal industry?

JODHI

No Sir, but I am sure I will be fine. I have a talent with people, and I am interested in the metal industry.

MR MCDONALD

I see. What is your background?

JODHI

I am a former pastor of a church in Carmel, California.

MR MCDONALD

That's interesting. Heaven knows I can do with some spiritual insight. My wife died recently, and, to be honest, my questions are more than the answers right now.

JODHI

Mr McDonald, I am incredibly sorry to hear of your loss.

MR MCDONALD

I appreciate your kind thoughts. Come and see me tomorrow morning at 10am, maybe we can help each other after all.

JODHI

That's great. Thank you for the opportunity.

MR MCDONALD

You are welcome. You sound like a good man, Jodhi. Let's talk more tomorrow.

JODHI

Thank you, Mr McDonald. Looking forward to seeing you tomorrow.

MR MCDONALD

Bye, Mr Livingstone.

JODHI

Bye, Mr McDonald.

Next scene

(It's the next day. Jodhi leaves the hotel for his interview. Jodhi arrives at Carnegie Scrap Metal dealers. Jodhi walks into reception.)

JODHI

Good morning Ma'am. A little something to say thank you for helping me yesterday. (*Jodhi hands her a box of chocolates.*)

RECEPTIONIST ANITA

Good morning Mr Livingstone. Thank you so much. That's very kind of you. I was just doing my job. *(blushing a little)*

JODHI

It's my pleasure. I recognised your South African accent the first time I spoke with you over the phone.

RECEPTIONIST ANITA

Good ear!

JODHI

You're the second person from South Africa that I have met in one week. God must be saying something to me. (*Jodhi is laughing and shaking his head.*)

RECEPTIONIST ANITA

Well, you also sound a bit South African.

JODHI

Guilty as charged! (*Hand raised*)
South African on my mother's side, but I was still in school when we moved to the US.

RECEPTIONIST ANITA

I hope you get the job then we will be 2 SAFFAS (*Subtitles*: "A colloquial expression for a person from South Africa") working here.

JODHI

I hope so too.

RECEPTIONIST ANITA

Mr McDonald is waiting for you in his office. Let me take you through to him.

JODHI

Thank you.

RECEPTIONIST ANITA

Mr McDonald, here is Mr Livingstone. It's a pleasure to introduce him.

MR MCDONALD

Thank you, Anita.

JODHI

(Jodhi greets Mr McDonald, and they shake hands.)

Pleased to meet you, Mr McDonald.

MR MCDONALD

Same here, Mr Livingstone. Please do take a seat.

JODHI

Thank you, Sir.

MR MCDONALD

So, the managerial position we have advertised is only available in 2 weeks' time. Mr Smith is retiring. He's 75, married to the job, never off sick in 50 years. He wants to step back but still plays a part in the company.
Maybe he could voluntarily mentor you a few hours a week? Show you the ropes kind of thing.

JODHI

That sounds perfect. If you would take a chance on me, I won't let you down.

MR MCDONALD

So, Mr Livingstone, tell me a bit more of yourself.

JODHI

Well, I recently got divorced, and I resigned from my work as a pastor in Carmel.

MR MCDONALD

Sorry to hear about that, Mr Livingstone. Could you tell me why did you resign?

JODHI

Let's just say that we had evangelical differences.

MR MCDONALD

Ok, I understand. Not everything in the church is always perfect.

JODHI

That's correct, Mr McDonald. People forget that church leaders are human too. They have their differences as well.

MR MCDONALD

So why enter the metal industry?

JODHI

Well, the life story of Lakshmi Mittal always inspired me, especially how he came from humble beginnings and ended up as the Steel Tycoon of our time. I also have an interest in shipbuilding.
I visited the site where they built the Titanic in Belfast. It's astonishing to see how much steel was involved in building it.

MR MCDONALD

Yeah, it's an interesting story. I was told my great grandfather provided some of the steel.

Well, Mr Livingstone, I am happy to give you a chance in my company. I have a good feeling about this. So, come Monday in 2 weeks' time, and we will start your training then.

JODHI

Many thanks, Mr McDonald. I really appreciate the opportunity. Oh, before I forget, I brought you a gift as well.

(He gifts him a book of Proverbs and a sympathy card and says goodbye.)

MR MCDONALD

Thank you, Mr Livingstone. I will read it. See you soon.

(They shake hands.)

JODHI

Goodbye, Mr McDonald. See you in 2 weeks when I report for duty.

MR MCDONALD

Goodbye, Mr Livingstone. Enjoy those two weeks off.

JODHI

Thanks.

(Jodhi is leaving while Mr McDonald is reading the card out loud to himself.)

"**Proverbs** kind of tell us that you become wise by walking with the wise. I am certain your wife was a child of the light who lit up the streets.

She must have had a heart that brought a smile to your face and filled your days with endless song. Remember her faithfulness, but especially remember her this way, lovely as an angel, beautiful as a rose. "

(A tear is running from Mr McDonald's eye.)

Next scene

(Jodhi arrives at his hotel. Jodhi greets Ruth, the receptionist.)

JODHI

Morning Ruth.

RUTH

Good morning Mr Livingstone. You look sparkling bright as a diamond!

JODHI

You, too, sparkle like a diamond as usual!

(Jodhi is winking at Ruth.)

RUTH

Oh, thanks, Mr Livingstone.

JODHI

Ruth, can you recommend a nice bar and restaurant? I feel like celebrating.

RUTH

Well, Mr Livingstone, there is a small bar/restaurant on Union Street. It's very popular. It's called the Candy Bar. I am sure you will enjoy it there.

JODHI

Sounds good. Could you book me a taxi for 8pm tonight to go there?

RUTH

Sure thing, Mr Livingstone. Stars are us.

(*Both laugh.*)

JODHI

Thanks, Ruth. Enjoy the rest of your twinkling day!

RUTH

Same to you, Mr Livingstone.

(*Both laugh.*)

(Jodhi takes the escalator to his room. Jodhi is in his room calling his children. Christian's phone is ringing.)

CHRISTIAN

Hello Dad.

JODHI

Hello Christian. How're things?

CHRISTIAN

Good Dad. How are things with you? Where are you now?

JODHI

I am doing well, Christian. I am in San Francisco. I just went for an interview this morning and got the job!

CHRISTIAN

That's great dad! What type of job is it?

JODHI

It's a managerial position at a scrap metal yard.

CHRISTIAN

That sounds good. When are we going to see you again?

JODHI

Let's say in 2 weeks' time at the weekend just before I start my work.

CHRISTIAN

That will be good. We are missing you.

JODHI

Missing you too. Can I speak with Jessica?

CHRISTIAN

Sure. Bye.

JODHI

Bye Christian.

JESSICA

Hello Dad. I love you more than words can say.

JODHI

Hello sweetheart. How's my sweet one?

JESSICA

Good.

JODHI

I am missing you guys. It hurts my heart. I will be there in a few weeks' time. How's your swimming going?

JESSICA

It's going well, but I have lost my goggles.

JODHI

That's a pity. They were very nice goggles. Don't worry, I will buy you even better ones.

JESSICA

Thanks, Dad.

JODHI

Ok, Jessica, I am going to go now. Love you lots, Lovey. Bye.

JESSICA

Ok, Dad. Love you lots too. Bye.

(*Jessica is crying.*)

JODHI

Bye Jessica.

(Jodhi is getting ready for the night. He showers and gets dressed. Reception is calling him. The taxi has arrived.)

ANTHOULA AT RECEPTION

Good evening Mr Livingstone. It's Anthoula here at reception. Your taxi has arrived.

JODHI

Thanks, Anthoula, I will be downstairs in a minute.

Next Scene

(*Jodhi is getting into the taxi.*)

TAXI DRIVER

Good evening Sir.

JODHI

Good evening. How's your night?

TAXI DRIVER

It's very busy tonight, Sir.

JODHI

Good, that's great for you!

TAXI DRIVER

Yes, Sir! I am happy-go-lucky. That's why I work for "Lucky Cabs, right".

(*The taxi driver is laughing.*)

(A song plays "I should be so Lucky" by Kylie Minogue.)

JODHI

Well, I hope I am lucky tonight.

(*Jodhi is smiling.*)

TAXI DRIVER

I am sure you will be. Everyone who meets me gets lucky.

(*The taxi driver is smiling.*)

(*Taxi arrives at the Candy Bar. Jodhi greets the taxi driver.*)

TAXI DRIVER

Here's the place, Sir. Good Luck.

JODHI

(Jodhi leaves the taxi.)

Thank you!

Next Scene

(Jodhi walks into Candy Bar on Union Street. He orders a glass of Bordeaux white wine at the bar.)

WAITRESS ELLEN

Good evening Sir. What can I get you?

JODHI

Which white wine do you have by the glass?

WAITRESS ELLEN

We have a Bordeaux Blanc from France by the glass.

JODHI

That will do. Can I have a large glass?

WAITRESS ELLEN

Sure. You can sit down. I will bring it to your table.

JODHI

Thanks!

(He sits outside at a small table with 2 chairs. He starts talking to a guy named John.)

JODHI

How's your night been?

JOHN

Relaxed. Just chilling out after seeing a client of mine.

JODHI

My name is Jodhi. Pleased to meet you. *(They shake hands.)*

JOHN

Nice to meet you too! I am John.

JODHI

That accent... is it Australian?

JOHN

Yeah, that's right. I am from Australia. I am just in town to see a client of mine.

JODHI

Ok, nice. You mentioned a client. What do you do for a living?

JOHN

I am in employment law.

JODHI

Interesting.

(2 girls walking down the stairs. Jodhi and John are smiling at each other.)

("Tonight is going to be a good night "plays by The Black-Eyed Peas.)

JOHN

Nice girls.

JODHI

Yeah, 100%.

(Ellen is coming to bring the glass of wine.)

WAITRESS ELLEN

Here is your wine. Super enjoy!

(The two girls sit down at a table next to the men. The one girl puts her handbag on the floor. A guy comes from behind and grabs her handbag, and runs away. Jodhi jumps up and runs after the guy and tackles him in the street. The handbag falls on the street. Jodhi grabs the handbag while the stranger is running off. The 2 girls and John are watching the scene. Jodhi is bringing the handbag to the girl. The girl is in shock. Jodhi gives the handbag back to the girl, and they introduce each other.)

JODHI

Here is your handbag.

HELEN

Thanks so much. I cannot believe what just happened!

JODHI

Don't worry. The "rope a dope " is gone.

HELEN

I am so thankful. How could I ever repay you?

JODHI

By having a drink with me.

(Jodhi is smiling.)

HELEN

Of course. What is your name?

JODHI

I am Jodhi.

HELEN

Nice to meet you, Jodhi. I am Helen.

(They both shake hands and kiss on the cheek.

JODHI

Nice to meet you, Helen. This is John.

HELEN

And you, John. This is my friend Jane.

JOHN

Nice to meet you, Jane.

JODHI

Helen, do you want to sit here then John can sit with Jane?

HELEN

Yeah sure, why not?

(John takes Helen's chair, and Helen sits next to Jodhi.)

JODHI

What drink can I get you?

HELEN

What are you drinking?

JODHI

A Bordeaux white.

HELEN

I would love to have the same. I love French whites.

JODHI

"Pouvez-vous parler francais?"
(*Subtitles*: "Can you speak french?")

HELEN

"Un peu"
(*Subtitles*: "A little bit")

JODHI

"Vous êtes belle"
(*Subtitles*: "You look beautiful")

HELEN

(Helen is blushing.)

"Merci"
(*Subtitles*: "Thanks")

(Jodhi is waving to the waitress Ellen to order a drink for Helen.)

WAITRESS ELLEN

Yes Sir. What can I get you?

JODHI

Could you please get this beautiful lady also a large Bordeaux white?

WAITRESS ELLEN

Of course, Sir.

JODHI

Thanks very much. Also, get her friend and John here anything they want.

WAITRESS ELLEN

Sure.

(Ellen takes John and Jane's order.)

JOHN

Thanks, mate.

JODHI

You are welcome, my friend.

HELEN

Are you always this generous?

JODHI

Well, it's nice to be nice.

HELEN

That's true.

JODHI

So, do you live here in San Francisco?

HELEN

I have just finished my studies here.

JODHI

Ok cool. What did you study?

HELEN

International Business Studies.

JODHI

That's a nice course.

HELEN

You have a different accent. Where are you from?

JODHI

Well, I grew up in South Africa but moved to the States when I was young.

HELEN

I love that accent; I can listen to it all day long.

JODHI

Shall I sing you a song of love?

(*Jodhi is smiling.*)

HELEN

Maybe! (*Helen is laughing.*) So, Jodhi, what do you do for a living?

JODHI

Well, I have just started out here. I have just recently got divorced and was a pastor of a church in Carmel.

HELEN

So sorry to hear about your marriage.
But hey, a Pastor? That's so cool!
Honestly – I haven't been in a church for a while...

(Helen is smiling)

JODHI

Same here. Well, at least for the last few days. *(Chuckle)* So, are you on holiday now, or are you going to start a job somewhere?

HELEN

I am taking a break for a while before looking for work.

JODHI

Me too. I am off for 2 weeks before I start my new position.

HELEN

What are you going to do?

JODHI

I am taking over the role of manager at Carnegie Scrap Metal.

HELEN

That's nice. Well, I just want to thank you again for getting my bag back. That was a heroic jump that you made on the guy.

JODHI

Yeah, well, that was a tackle in rugby, so I thought it was the only way to stop the guy.

HELEN

What is rugby?

JODHI

It's like American football, except it's more physical. I played it in South Africa at school.

HELEN

Well, I am forever grateful to you. You know there was a very expensive necklace in my handbag. It has a Tanzanite stone. I got it from my grandmother. Sometimes I carry it with me.

JODHI

So, what was the special occasion tonight?

HELEN

Well, I suppose meeting you!

(*They both are laughing.*)

JODHI

I am glad I could save it for you.

HELEN

Yeah, seriously, I had it in my bag tonight because Jane and I are going to meet another friend of ours – She is from Tanzania, and I wanted to show her the necklace.

JODHI

I heard Tanzanites are only mined in Tanzania. Is that correct?

HELEN

Yes, it's true. That's what makes them special. They are very rare stones these days. Rarer than beauty itself!

JODHI

Well, the owner of the necklace looks like she is also very rare and special. Like I said before, a gift of natural beauty herself!

HELEN

(Helen is blushing.)

Well, you have the gift of Encanto, I see.

JODHI

Si.

(Jodhi is smiling.)

HELEN

I was thinking of repaying you for your heroic deed. I want to invite you for a BBQ at my family ranch this weekend. We have horses too!

JODHI

That's a splendid idea. Coming from South Africa, I am crazy about doing a BBQ. They call it a "Braai" in South Africa.

HELEN

That's great, then! Give me your number. I will give you a text over the weekend.

(Jodhi is giving Helen his number.)

HELEN

Ok, I am going to have to leave now. It was nice chatting with you. See you at the weekend.

JODHI

It was my pleasure. See you.

(They give each other a hug.)

HELEN

Jane, shall we go? Darlene is waiting for us at Moongate Lounge.

JANE

Ok. Goodbye John. Nice to meet you. Also, you, Jodhi and thanks for the drink!

JOHN

You are welcome. Take care.

JODHI

Bye, enjoy your night.

(The two girls are walking off.)

JODHI

They seem like two really nice girls.

JOHN

Yeah, they do. You look very happy meeting Helen.

JODHI

Yes, she is a great girl. (*Smiling*) I probably also have to go now. Nice meeting you, mate. Take my number. Call me anytime then we can go for a drink again.

(John is taking Jodi's number.)

JOHN

Cheers, mate, it was nice to meet you too. Take care.

(Jodhi is walking to the bar to pay his bill.)

JODHI

Hi, I just want to pay for my drink and of course a tip for you!

ELLEN WAITRESS

Thanks, that is kind of you! I see you got lucky tonight!

JODHI

(Jodhi is smiling.)

I guess so. I need all the luck at this stage of my life.

(Jodhi is tapping his phone on the card machine.)

ELLEN WAITRESS

Hope to see you here again!

JODHI

Thank you. Bye.

ELLEN WAITRESS

Bye-bye.

(Jodhi is walking off to get a taxi to his hotel.)

76

Bye-bye.

(Jodhi is walking off to get a taxi to his hotel.)

Next Scene

(It's Saturday morning. Jodhi is in his hotel room. He gets a text from Helen inviting him to come to her family home at 3pm in the afternoon. He is replying back to her.)

TEXT FROM HELEN

Good morning Jodhi! Hope you are doing well. Do you want to come at 3pm today for a BBQ?

TEXT FROM JODHI

Hi Helen! That will be great. Please send me your address, and I will be there.

TEXT FROM HELEN

6 GREEN FIELDS FARM, SANTA CRUZ COUNTY. Be there or be square. Hahaha.

TEXT FROM JODHI

You bet I will be there. See you at 3pm.

(Jodhi is getting ready to go to Helen. Jodhi goes to reception. He greets Ruth at reception.)

JODHI

Good afternoon Ruth.

RUTH

Good afternoon Mr Livingstone. How was your night at Candy Bar?

JODHI

It was perfect. Thank you, Ruth. I met a girl, and she invited me today to her family's farm. Togetherness is a magical thing.

RUTH

Wow. I am happy for you!

JODHI

Thank you. I am glad you suggested the Candy Bar to me.

RUTH

I hope my suggestion brought you good fortune.

JODHI

It definitely seems so! Looks like my taxi has just arrived.

RUTH

Well, have a lovely afternoon Mr Livingstone.

JODHI

Thank you, Ruth. Talk with you soon.

(Jodhi goes outside to get his taxi.)

(*"Bring the Old Town "plays by Lil Nas X & Billy Ray Cyrus*)

(Jodhi arrives at the Farm. He is walking away from the taxi. Jodhi is carrying a bunch of white lilies and a bunch of white roses. It's a beautiful farm with lots of horses and some sheep. Helen is coming out to meet him.)

HELEN

Good afternoon Pastor! *(Helen is smiling.)*

JODHI

Good afternoon Helen! What a beautiful day! These lilies are for you.

HELEN

Thank you, Jodhi!

(Helen is giving Jodhi a hug.)

Anyway, come in. Let me introduce you to the family.

(They walk into the house.)

HELEN'S MUM

(Helen's mum greets Jodhi.)

Hello, you must be Helen's hero. She told us the whole story. *(smiling)*

JODHI

(Jodhi is smiling and shaking Helen's mother's hand.)

Glad to meet you. It was my honour to be her hero.

(Jodhi gives her white roses.)

HELEN'S MUM

Thank you very much, Jodhi. They smell very nice!
Let's go to the garden – the rest of the family is there.

(The family sit around a table in the back garden.)

HELEN

Hi guys, this is Jodhi. Jodhi, this is my family. That's my dad, Robert,
my brother David and then that's Becca, my younger sister.

JODHI

What a nice family. My pleasure to meet you.

HELEN'S DAD

Nice to meet you too, Jodhi. I feel I know you already. Sit down and
make yourself comfortable.

JODHI

(Jodhi and Helen are sitting down next to each other.)

Thank you.

HELEN'S DAD

I heard you are the king of BBQs, the BBQ supreme.

JODHI

Sure, I have my moments. *(Jodhi is smiling.)*

HELEN'S DAD

Well, we are doing lamb chops today. As you can see, we have a lot of sheep on the farm. (*Helen's dad is smiling.)*

JODHI

That will be great. I love Lamb chops.

HELEN'S DAD

Well, that's good then. Helen told us you grew up in South Africa and that you like South African white wine.

JODHI

Yeah, I grew up amongst the wine farms in the Western Cape. You can take the man out of the town but not the Cape. *(Smiling)*

HELEN'S DAD

Well, Mr Cape Crusader *(laughing),* we have bought you a Sauvignon Blanc from Durbanville Hills wine farm in the Cape. Do you know it?

JODHI

Yeah, it's very close to where I grew up! Wow, thank you very much. I appreciate that. They produce some of the finest wines in the world.

HELEN'S DAD

Yeah, I also like their wine. It's a winner all day long. Sit down and make yourself comfortable.

JODHI

Thanks.

HELEN'S DAD

So Jodhi, tell us, how did you end up in the USA?

JODHI

Well, my father got a transfer via our church in South Africa to be a pastor at a church in Montana in the Rocky Mountains.

HELEN'S DAD

Is your father still there?

JODHI

No, unfortunately, he died in a car crash near Salinas on his way to visit me in Carmel-by- the Sea.

HELEN'S DAD

Very sorry to hear about that.

JODHI

That's ok. It's been a few years now.

HELEN'S MOTHER

Is your mother still in Montana?

JODHI

No, she moved back to South Africa. She has remarried a Brit.

HELEN'S MOTHER

Oh, that's good, so at least she is not alone anymore.

JODHI

Yeah, the family all get on well with him.

HELEN'S DAD

So, Helen told me that you also have been a pastor.

JODHI

Yeah, I was a pastor in a church in Carmel-by- the Sea. San Francisco, this is a fresh start for me. It's all new to me. I didn't want to be too far away from my children.

HELEN'S DAD

I understand. How many children do you have?

JODHI

I have a boy and a girl. Christian and Jessica.

HELEN'S MUM

Those are beautiful names. You must bring them here one day. We have a lot of horses. Maybe they would like to go on the horses.

JODHI

I am sure they will. Horses are the fast way to the future. *(laughing)*

HELEN'S MUM

Yes, Helen, don't you want to take Jodhi to show him the horses of the future. *(smiling)*

HELEN

Sure, Mum.

(Jodhi and Helen are walking on the farm to the horse stables.)

HELEN

So, Jodhi, if you don't mind me asking – what happened between you and your ex-wife?

JODHI

We just had a lot of arguments over the years. It happens. She eventually decided she wanted her own freedom. She gave me the divorce papers, and I eventually signed them.

HELEN

Sorry to hear that, Jodhi. Although it is a difficult thing to go through, I think things happen for a reason.

JODHI

Yes, I agree. Some people are meant to be just friends, while I believe there is someone that just fits with you, and you can build your dream with that person.

HELEN

Ditto. I am also believing like that.

(Helen and Jodhi are reaching the horse stables.)

(Helen shows Jodhi her white horse called Aurora.)

HELEN

So Jodhi, this is my horse called Aurora. I got her when I turned 16.

JODHI

She is beautiful. Did you name her Aurora because of the Sleeping Beauty story?

(Jodhi is smiling.)

HELEN

You are right! I have loved that story since my mother read it to me as a 3-year-old.

JODHI

Well, maybe you are meant to be a princess. *(Jodhi is laughing.)*

HELEN

Let's go back. I think they might have started the BBQ or "braai", as you say.

JODHI

Ok. I am looking forward to it.

(Jodhi and Helen are back at the BBQ.)

DAVID

So Jodhi, I heard you like rugby?

JODHI

Yeah, I played in South Africa. Almost every boy in South Africa plays rugby in school.

DAVID

I suppose you also like American football.

JODHI

Yeah, for sure.

DAVID

What team do you support?

JODHI

The New York Giants.

DAVID

Good team to support. What about baseball?

JODHI

San Francisco Giants all the way.

DAVID

It looks like you support all the teams that have the name Giants in the name. (*David is laughing*)

JODHI

It looks like it. The funny thing is I always had this dream to open a rugby club in Edinburgh, Scotland, even though I don't live there. I want to call it the Braveheart Giants. (*Jodhi smiling*)

DAVID

How so?

JODHI

I am half Scottish. I think it will be great to have a team half Scottish and half South African. They will be true Warriors, no better combination than the William Wallace troops and South African "Bittereinders" together in one rugby team. They will be unbeatable.

DAVID

What does "Bittereinders" mean?

JODHI

They were Boer guerrilla fighters in the Second Boer War and were the last to give up the fight before the English took us over. I even have a shotgun from the Second Boer War that my late grandfather gave to me before he died.

HELEN'S DAD

That's interesting. Has Helen told you that I make equipment and gear for rifles?

JODHI

That's a surprise – no, we haven't gone that far in our conversations. (*Jodhi is laughing.*)

HELEN'S DAD

Well, next time, we can have a more in-depth conversation about that. But for now, it looks like the meat is ready.

JODHI

Wow. It looks "Lekker"
(*Subtitles*: "delicious")

BECCA HELLEN SISTER

What does "lekker" mean?

JODHI

It means delicious in Afrikaans.

BECCA HELEN SISTER

Jodhi. you must teach us more Afrikaans words, then I can show off in front of my friends in school.

HELEN

That will be cool, hey Becca.

BECCA

Yeah, plus it is the coolest accent.

JODHI

No problem. I will teach you a few sentences.

HELEN'S DAD

So Jodhi, next time is your turn to make us a nice "Braai" (*Subtitles*: "Barbeque").

JODHI

That will be my pleasure.

HELEN'S DAD

So, everyone, help yourself. Bon appétit!
(Subtitles: "Enjoy your meal")

(They all enjoy their meal. The night ends. Jodhi says goodbye to the family.)

JODHI

Thanks very much for the day. It was great meeting you all.

HELEN'S DAD

You are very welcome. We hope to see you soon again.

HELEN

Let me show you the Rose Garden before you phone your taxi.

JODHI

That will be nice.

(Helen takes Jodhi to the Rose Garden.)

JODHI

Wow, I didn't know you had a Rose Garden. Otherwise, I would have bought another type of flower instead of roses.

HELEN

No, my mother likes all kinds of roses. That was a good gift to her. Thanks also for my lilies, that's my favourite flower.

JODHI

You are welcome. You are becoming my favourite person.
(Jodhi is smiling.)

HELEN

Awhh, thanks, Jodhi. I think I am starting to like you too.
(Helen is smiling and blushing.)

(Jodhi looks Helen in the eyes and kisses her.)

JODHI

I better phone my taxi.

HELEN

Ok.

JODHI

Thanks for a truly wonderful day with your family.

HELEN

No problem. I can see they like you.

JODHI

That's nice to know.

HELEN

You have my number. Call me any time.

JODHI

I sure will, Helen.

(They both hug. Jodhi is phoning the taxi.)

(Jodhi arrives at his hotel. Jodhi goes to bed. He again starts getting a dream about a rider on a white horse with a bow in his hand trying to conquer. He also sees a black horse and an economic collapse in the Stock Market in New York. He sees how people are using a global cryptocurrency and how people are using their hands to buy and sell things.)

Next Scene

(Jodhi calls Helen. Helen picks up the phone.)

HELEN

Good morning Jodhi.

JODHI

Good morning Helen. I think a star is born.

HELEN

Yes, I have a twinkle in my eye.

(Helen is smiling.)

JODHI

(Jodhi laughs.)

Thank you for yesterday. It was greater than good. I bet you were on a training course for the great. (*They both laugh.*)

HELEN

Of course.

(Helen is smiling.)

JODHI

Listen, I was thinking, I want to go to New York for a holiday before I start my new job. Do you want to join me?

HELEN

I would love to. When are you thinking about going?

JODHI

Maybe on Tuesday.

HELEN

Sounds good. It gives me 2 days to pack my bags. You are my number one. *(Helen smiles.)*

JODHI

Better than being number 2. (*They both laugh*.) Great. I will book it today for Tuesday.

HELEN

Greater than great. I am excited.

JODHI

Me too. Speak to you soon.

HELEN

Ok. Have a good day!

JODHI

You too!

HELEN

Lovey bye.

JODHI

Lovey, lovey bye.

Next scene

(It's Tuesday morning. Jodhi is checking out of the hotel and says goodbye to Ruth.)

JODHI

Morning Ruth.

RUTH

Morning Mr Livingstone. It seems you had a great stay at our hotel. A lot of things have happened for good to you!

JODHI

Very true. God is good. *(Jodhi is smiling)*

RUTH

Yes, all the time! Your taxi is ready. It was a real pleasure having you here.

JODHI

I enjoyed it here. Thanks for the advice to go to Candy Bar. It worked out perfect!

RUTH

You are welcome. She is a lucky girl.

JODHI

I think I am a lucky guy. Bye, God bless.

RUTH

Goodbye, Mr Livingstone.

(Song plays "She drives me crazy" by Fine Young Cannibals)

(Jodhi is going to his taxi. He gets into his taxi and phone Helen. The phone is ringing. She answers the phone)

HELEN

Good morning Mr Charming.

JODHI

Good morning Sleeping beauty.

HELEN

I am more like Cinderella. *(She laughs.)*

JODHI

I wholeheartedly agree with that one. Listen, I am in the taxi now. Where are you?

HELEN

I am in the car with my father. We are close to the airport now.

JODHI

Good. I will be at the airport in 20 min.

HELEN

I can hardly wait. My heart is beating fast.

JODHI

Don't worry, I am moving fast. *(Jodhi smiles.)*

HELEN

See you soon!

JODHI

Ok sweetheart.

Next Scene

(The taxi is arriving at the airport. Jodhi goes into the airport. Texting Helen.)

JODHI TEXTING HELEN

I am here in the queue at the American Airlines check-in point.

HELEN

I am just here behind you. *(smiling)*

(They hug and kiss each other.)

JODHI

Glad to see you.

HELEN

I am excited. I feel like dancing.

JODHI

Me too. I feel the rhythm.

(They reach the front of the queue. A lady called Jade is serving them at the Front desk.)

JADE AT THE FRONT DESK

Morning Sir. Mr Livingstone, I presume?

(Jade is smiling.)

JODHI

How did you know my surname?

97

JADE

Your name is on your luggage tag, Sir. It was a no-brainer.
(*Jade is smiling.*)

(*Jade and Jodhi are both smiling. Jade is looking up Jodhi's booking on the system.*)

Ok, I see you have booked 2 tickets.

JODHI

That's right the other ticket is for Miss Helen Taylor.

JADE

Ok. It seems that you guys are in luck. The plane is not full. We have a special today. You can upgrade both of your tickets for $50 each to go, business class. Do you want to do that?

JODHI

(*Jodhi is looking at Helen and smiling.*)

That will be amazing, thanks.

JADE

Ok, great, that's you checked in now.

(Jodhi and Helen are sitting in business class. Enjoying a glass of Champagne and Oysters.)

(A song plays "Take me anywhere "by Rita Ora.)

HELEN

I like this song. I was actually born in LA. We lived there for 8 years.

JODHI

That's interesting. We should go there together one day.

HELEN

That will be great.

(Helen is holding Jodhi's hand.)

JODHI

Let's open the champagne.

HELEN

Yeah, let's pop the cork and get the bubbles going.

JODHI

Yes, this is life. I always had it in my heart to be a high flyer in business class and have my woman by my side.

HELEN

That's so sweet of you to say that! I always dreamed about that lifestyle too! That's why I studied International Business.

(Jodhi and Helen are kissing.)

Next Scene in New York

*(Jodhi and Helen arrive at JFK Airport in New York. They take a taxi to the Hilton hotel in Manhattan. The song plays '**New York New York' by Frank Sinatra** as they drive through Manhattan to The Hilton Garden Inn on Pearl Street. They arrive at the hotel.)*

TAXI DRIVER

This is your hotel, Sir.

JODHI

Thank you.

(Jodhi is getting the suitcases out and waves to the taxi driver. They enter the hotel.)

VANESSA AT RECEPTION

Good morning Sir. What is your name?

JODHI

My name is Jodhi Livingstone.

VANESSA AT RECEPTION

Ok, let me see. You booked for 2 people. Your room is Room 28 on the 4th floor. *(Vanessa gives him the keys.)*

JODHI

Thanks. I was wondering, do you perhaps know of anyone that is knowledgeable in trading that can give us a short drive around the financial district tomorrow morning?

VANESSA

Sure. Actually, my cousin Vinnie I am sure he will do it. He has a friend Jordan who studies with him. Jordan knows everything about the stock market. They are both on a holiday break. If you can give them a tip, students will do anything for some money.

JODHI

Deal. Thanks. Could you please ask him to be here at 9 am? Then afterwards, if he can take us to the Jane Hotel. That would be great. I have made a booking there for tomorrow.

VANESSA

Sure, no problem. I will give him a call and let you know soon.

JODHI AND HELEN

Thank you!

(Jodhi and Helen take the elevator to their floor. As they enter the room, they start kissing and fall down on the bed. They look each other in the eye. They whisper into each other's ears.)

JODHI

Thank you for coming with me. You are simply the greatest.

HELEN

Thank you for inviting me. You are not so bad either. *(Helen laughs.)*

(Vanessa is phoning from Reception. Jodhi picks up.)

JODHI

Hi

VANESSA

It's Vanessa here from reception. I spoke with Vinnie. He and Jordan
are available to show you around tomorrow to see some sites. They
will be at the reception at 9am in the morning.

JODHI

Splendid! Thanks, Vanessa. I owe you big time!

VANESSA

You are welcome. Have a good night!

Next Scene

(Jodhi and Helen go to bed. They fall asleep in each other's arms.)

(Jodhi has another dream about the rider on a white horse that he saw in his previous dream. He looks closer at the rider's face, and he looks like he is from the Middle East. He sees a dragon and a beast coming out of the Sea. He sees the United Nations building in New York. He also sees a beast coming out of the Earth. He sees the Vatican and the Pope. It supports the first Beast of the sea. He wakes up. Get some water. It's early morning. Helen is waking up. He tells Helen that he had a vivid dream.)

HELEN

Morning. Why are you awake so early?

JODHI

I had a scary dream.

HELEN

About what?

JODHI

It was about a beast coming out of the sea and a beast out of the earth, like in the book of Revelation. This is not the first time that I have had a dream about the book of Revelation. I had 3 dreams before, and this is the 4th dream.

HELEN

There must be a reason why you are getting these dreams ?

JODHI

Yeah there must be. Let's sleep a bit more. (*They cuddle and spoon.*)

HELEN

Ok.

Next Scene

(Later, Jodhi and Helen wake up.)

JODHI

Good morning beautiful.

HELEN

Good morning handsome.

(They kiss each other.)

JODHI

Do you want to go for a shower first? In half an hour, the guys will be here.

HELEN

Yes, sure, honey. Thanks for being a true gentleman.

(Helen is smiling.)

Next Scene

(They get ready. Vanessa phones from Reception. They take their suitcases and go downstairs to meet Vinnie and Jordan at reception.)

VANESSA

Morning! Did you two have a good sleep?

JODHI

Like Angels.

(Jodhi is smiling.)

VANESSA

Mr Livingstone this is my cousin Vinnie and his friend Jordan.

JODHI

Like my cousin Vinnie in the movie! (*Everybody laughs.)*

(They all greet each other and say goodbye to Vanessa.)

JODHI

Great! Let's go. Bye Vanessa. Thanks for getting these two guys. They seem smarter than Pumba and Timon in Lion King.

(Everybody laughs.)

VANESSA

You are welcome, Mr Livingstone. I am sure you are going to have a good time with them. They are the best in the west. Every Simba needs a Pumba and Timon.

(Vanessa is smiling.)

JODHI

I am sure.

(Vinnie and Jordan are taking the suitcases into the car. They all get in the car. Vinnie is in the driving seat, and Jordan is in the front passenger seat. Jodhi and Helen are in the back seat.)

VINNIE

So, Mr Livingstone, where do you want me to take you first?

JODHI

As we are very close to the Charging Bull statue, could you please take us there first?

VINNIE

Sure, no problem Mr Livingstone! Let's go, go.

JODHI

Thanks, Vinnie. So, Jordan, I heard that you are a very ardent student of the stock market.

JORDAN

Yes, I am for sure! Ask me anything about it, and I will tell you the answer.

JODHI

What do you think? Is the current market very bullish?

JORDAN

No, sir, it is very unstable. I am sure we are heading for a massive crash bigger than 1929.

JODHI

Why do you say that?

JORDAN

It's because of the uncertainty in the economic market today.

(They drive next to the charging bull.)

VINNIE

Right here is the Charging Bull.

(Vinnie pointing the statue by driving past.)

JODHI

Wow, it's such an iconic statue. Can you just stop for a moment so that we can take a picture?

VINNIE

Yes, sure.

(Vinnie stops the car for a few seconds.)

JODHI

Helen, can you please take a picture of the bull.

HELEN

Yes, love.

(Helen's window is next to the Charging Bull. She is taking a picture of the Charging Bull.)

JODHI

Does anyone know the background of the Charging Bull?

VINNIE

Sure, we covered that in one of our classes in our studies.

JODHI

Can you share it with us a bit?

VINNIE

No problem. The sculpture was created by Italian artist Arturo Di Modica in the wake of the 1987 Black Monday stock market crash. In the late evening of December 14, 1989, Di Modica arrived on Wall Street with the Charging Bull on the back of a truck and illegally dropped the sculpture outside of the New York Stock Exchange Building.
After being removed by the New York City Police Department later that day, the Charging Bull was installed here at Bowling Green on December 20, 1989.

JODHI

Wow, that's very interesting, Vinnie. I give you 10 out of 10 for that.

VINNIE

Thanks, Sir. You are much more gracious than my lecturers.

(Everybody laughs.)

JODHI

You are welcome, Vinnie. Could we move on to The New York Stock Exchange before someone crashes into our car?

(Jodhi is smiling.)

VINNIE

Sure Sir.

(They are driving towards The New York Stock Exchange building.)

JODHI

So, Jordan, do you always follow the stock market on a daily basis?

JORDAN

Yes. You know, The Federal Reserve Bank has made an announcement that they are going to put interest rates up today, but they haven't confirmed how much.

JODHI

Will that influence the stock market a lot?

JORDAN

Yes, for sure, for it has an immediate effect on the stock market, especially if there is a huge increase in the interest rates. Let me check what's happening in the market right now.

(Jordan is checking on his phone.)

(A song plays in the background, "Stock Market Rap" by Smart Songs.)

VINNIE

We are almost at the New York Stock Exchange building.

JODHI

That's brilliant.

JORDAN

(Jordan is looking on his phone.)

Oh, my goodness!!!

JODHI

What's happening?

JORDAN

There is a major crash in the Stock Market! Vinnie, could you please switch the radio on to the news channel.

VINNIE

Yes, no problem.

(Vinnie puts the channel on Fox news. A Major announcement is commencing. The Stock Market has fallen to a record-breaking low. Every stock and share are influenced, even crypto currencies.)

(They arrive at the New York Stock Exchange building, and Vinnie parks the car.)

(A scene in the building on the trading floor follows. The traders are in shock. They are all over the place.)

JORDAN

This is mega mad. It's like your biggest tsunami ever on the stock market!!
(They sit in awe.)

JODHI

Jordan, have you invested any money in the stock market?

JORDAN

Luckily not a lot, I am still a student, so I haven't much money to invest.

(Jordan is laughing.)

JODHI

But you sure know the game. I am going to call you Jordan Belfort alias Wolf of Wall street from now on.

(They all laugh in the car.)

VINNIE

Mr Livingstone, where shall we go next?

JODHI

Can you please take us to the One World Trade Centre?

VINNIE

As you wish, Mr Livingstone.

JODHI

So, Jordan, do you have anything you can tell us about the Twin Towers that were there before the One World Trade Centre was destroyed?

JORDAN

Of course. Did you know that the Port of New York had decided to use a new version of the city building code that did not require as many staircases as the earlier edition?

Instead of six staircases, including a specially reinforced fire escape, the trade centre had three stairs in each tower. So, therefore, if they had gone with the original version, much more people would have escaped from the 9/11 attack.

JODHI

Wow. It sounds almost like the Titanic. The same thing happened. During the design stage, the chief draughtsman submitted a plan to provide 64 lifeboats, but they ended up with only 20 because they felt that the deck would be too cluttered.

HELEN

That's so sad.

JODHI

Yeah, imagine - most of those people's lives on the Titanic could have been saved if they went with his plan. All lives matter. They were in it together. Think of the grandchildren to be that were lost.

JORDAN

I see what you mean about a historical human tragedy and a lot of similarities between the Titanic and the Twin Towers.

VINNIE

Yeah, my mother told me how devastating it was. She was working as a waitress at a coffee shop in the Financial District. They all had to run for their lives.

JORDAN

I remember I was still very small. I saw it on TV live. It was breaking news.

VINNIE

Guys, we are here. There is the One World Trade Centre.

(They stop for a moment and look at the One World Trade Centre.)

HELEN

Wow, it's very tall.

JORDAN

Yeah, they made it deliberately 1776 ft in reference to the year when the United States Declaration of Independence was signed.

JODHI

That's a very interesting fact. Do you know that Adam Smith published the Wealth of Nations in the same year, 1776, on the 9th of March?

JORDAN

That makes all sense now. It can't be by accident that it was the same year of the USA's independence.

JODHI

No. Like the wise Master turtle in Kung Fu Panda movie would say, there are no things such as accidents.

VINNIE

Wise words.

(They are all laughing.)

JODHI

Jordan, what do you think? Will this building still stand for many years to come?

JORDAN

Well, I think if history has taught us one thing, it is that we can never be too confident.

JODHI

That's probably the best thing you have said today. You are getting wiser by the minute. It seems you are learning from the Master.

(*They are all laughing.*)

Right guys, I think we have seen what we wanted to see. Vinnie, could you please take us to the Jane hotel.

VINNIE

Sure.

Next Scene

(They all get into the car and drive to the Jane Hotel.)

JODHI

Let me tell you about this hotel that we are going to. It was the original place where the survivors of the Titanic slept overnight when they reached New York.

HELEN

That's very interesting. You are always full of surprises.

JODHI

Yeah, I have a few more surprises today.

(Jodhi is smiling.)

HELEN

I can't wait.

(Helen is giving Jodhi a kiss.)

JORDAN

You two lovebirds are making me shy.

VINNIE

Jordan, don't be jealous. It's high time that you get yourself a girlfriend.

JORDAN

I am waiting… she is out there!

JODHI

That's the spirit, Jordan. Keep the faith!

HELEN

So, tell us more about the hotel we are going to.

JODHI

Well, it's very close to PIER 54, where the rescue ship of the Titanic, the RMS Carpathia, anchored in New York. The building was originally the American Seaman's Friend Society Sailors' Home and Institute at the time of the sinking of the Titanic.

VINNIE

Wow, and when was it changed into a hotel?

JODHI

They renovated the place, I think, in 2008, and made it into a proper hotel. The rooms are like cabins in a boat as a reminder of the rescue ship. The RMS Carpathia. They modernised it even more. Apparently, the hotel is run by Robots.

HELEN

Wow.

JODHI

I have a grand idea. Why don't you two join us for a meal at The Frying Pan? We haven't eaten yet. The meal will be on me.

VINNIE

That sounds great!

JORDAN

Yeah, that will be brilliant. I am starving.

JODHI

Deal.

VINNIE

Well, we have just arrived at the Jane Hotel.

JODHI

Ok, let's check-in and then go for a meal.

VINNIE

Sure, we will help with the suitcases. We are on the case.

Next Scene

(They all get out of the car. Vinnie and Jordan are helping with the suitcases.)

(They are entering the Jane hotel. A robot helps them at the desk.)

ROBOT JANE

Good morning. How can I help you?

JODHI

We are here to check-in.

ROBOT JANE

Great. What is your surname?

JODHI

Mr Livingstone.

ROBOT JANE

Confirmed cabin for 2 ready. Take keys. (*Keys come out of the machine.*)

Cabin 418 on the 4th floor. Take the escalator on the right.

JODHI

Thank you.

ROBOT JANE

Thank you. Enjoy your stay.

JORDAN

That's so amazing. I like this type of technology.

JODHI

I still prefer the human touch. (*Jodhi is giving Helen a hug.*)

(*They all go upstairs by lift to the 4th floor.*)

(*They enter the Cabin. It looks very modern. There are 2 small champagne bottles on the desk.*)

HELEN

Wow, this is a nice cabin.

JODHI

The bed is still smaller than usual, but I don't complain. I like to snuggle up to you.

HELEN

I know you do. (*Helen is blushing.*)

Jordan and Vinnie are putting the suitcases down.

JODHI

Ok guys, let's go for a nice meal.

VINNIE

Ok marvellous.

Next Scene

(They get into the car. Driving to the Frying pan restaurant. They pass Pier 54, where the Carpathia anchored.)

JODHI

That's Pier 54, where the RMS Carpathia anchored the night they arrived in New York.

VINNIE

Wow, I have lived all my life in New York and never knew that.

JODHI

You are never old enough to learn. *(Jodhi is laughing.)*

VINNIE

I guess so.

(They drive to Pier 66 to The Frying Pan restaurant.)

HELEN

So Jodhi, the restaurant you are taking us to. Why did you choose this one?

JODHI

Well, I chose this restaurant because it has a great history.

HELEN

Not because of the food. *(Helen is smiling.)* Tell us about it.

121

JODHI

Of course, the food is great! It's a boat restaurant. It was built in 1929. The Lightship was in service for over 30 years before being relieved of duty. She was brought to New York City in 1989 and became a "hidden gem" of New York nightlife.

JORDAN

Now I understand you. It was the same year of the 1929 Stock Market Crash.

JODHI

You know Jordan. I already like you. You are sharp as a razor. You were right. I can ask you anything about Wall Street. You know it. *(They are all laughing.)*

VINNIE

Well, guys, we are here. Let me park the car.

Next Scene

(Vinnie parks the car. They all get out of the car. They enter the boat and go to sit at one of the tables outside. The waiter Pierre arrives to give them menus.)

WAITER PIERRE

Hello Guys, my name is Pierre. I am your waiter for today.

JODHI

Pierre, you sound French. Are you from the City of Love? *(Jodhi is smiling.)*

PIERRE

Oui, viva la France! (subtitles: "Yes, viva France")

JODHI

Fruits de mer? (subtitles: "sea food"?)

PIERRE

Plateau fruits de mer for 4? (subtitles: "seafood platter" for 4?)

JODHI

Sounds good, and bring us a jug of water too, please.

PIERRE

Sure.

(Pierre goes to place the order.)

JORDAN

They have done a good job on this boat, considering how old it is.

JODHI

Yes. It's a great idea. You know, the oldest actual active ocean-faring passenger ship they turned into a luxury hotel.

JORDAN

What is the name of the ship?

JODHI

The MV Doulos Phos. It was built in 1914, around 2 years after the sinking of the Titanic.

VINNIE

Where did they build it?

JODHI

They built it in Newport, Virginia. It was first called SS Medina. It was eventually sold by an Italian company to a Christian missionary organisation that used it for 32 years as a floating Christian bookshop. It went to all the nations of the world. It ended up in Indonesia, where they renovated it into a hotel.

HELEN

That's very interesting. We should visit it one day.

JODHI

Yeah, I would like to.

(Pierre comes back with the food.)

PIERRE

Here is your food, guys.

JODHI

Thanks, it looks delicious.

(They all eat. The night is finished. Vinnie takes them to their hotel. They say goodbye.)

JODHI

Well, guys, it was a real pleasure to meet you guys. New York in 80 minutes! (*They all laugh.*) Send me your account details, and I will transfer some money to both of you.

(They shake hands with each other and say goodbye. Jodhi and Helen go into the Jane hotel.)

Next Scene

(A song plays in the background, "International Love" by Pitbull.)

JODHI

Looking forward to that champagne now.

HELEN

Me too!

(They are taking the lift to the 4th floor and getting into the cabin. They are giving each other a hug and then sitting down on the cabin beds.)

JODHI

Let me pour us some champagne.

HELEN

That will be lovely, lovely.

JODHI

Here you go. Let's toast to us.

HELEN

Yes, to us. May we be blessed as a couple!

JODHI

To our future!
(Clinking glasses.)

HELEN

So Jodhi, tell me more about the dreams you had.

JODHI

Ok, I will. The first dream speaks about 4 horses, and each horse represents something in the time we are heading for. I think why the dreams come so frequently is because we are very close to that time, and people need to be made aware of it so that they are prepared when it happens.

HELEN

Tell me, what does each horse represent?

JODHI

The first one is the white horse…

(Jodhi is reading to Helen on his phone. In Revelation 6:1-2)

"I watched as the Lamb opened the first of the seven seals. Then I heard one of the four living creatures say in a voice like thunder, "Come!" I looked, and there before me was a white horse! Its rider held a bow, and he was given a crown, and he rode out as a conqueror bent on conquest."

The interpretation of that is it represents the Anti-Christ. He will look like he is a man of peace. That's why he is on a white horse. It refers to the 7-year peace treaty that was signed in 2033 in the Middle East. That peace treaty will be broken in the middle of the 7 years by the Anti-Christ himself. That means 18 months from now.

Now you understand why these dreams come so frequently.

HELEN

I don't quite get it. Who is the Lamb referring to here?

JODHI

It refers to Jesus. He is the only One that can open the seals. That means He is the One that gives us the revelation of the events that will take place?

HELEN

Who wrote the Book of Revelation?

JODHI

It is written by John the Apostle. He was one of Jesus's 12 disciples. He was the last of the 12 disciples to die, and this was the last book he wrote on the Isle of Patmos.

HELEN

Ok, tell me about the second horse.

JODHI

(Jodhi is reading. Revelation 6:3-4)

"When the Lamb opened the second seal, I heard the second living creature say, "Come!" [4] Then another horse came out, a fiery red one. Its rider was given the power to take peace from the earth and to make people kill each other. To him was given a large sword."

The second horse speaks about the military leader of the Anti-Christ who is executing people that will not follow the Anti-Christ.

HELEN

Is that the Great Tribulation the Bible speaks of?

JODHI

That's correct. You are clever *(Jodhi is smiling)* So, the Great Tribulation starts when the Anti-Christ breaking the 7-year peace treaty.

HELEN

Ok, I understand. What about the 3rd horse?

JODHI

(Jodhi is reading. Revelation 6: 5-6)

"When the Lamb opened the third seal, I heard the third living creature say, "Come!" I looked, and there before me was a black horse! Its rider was holding a pair of scales in his hand. ^{6} Then I heard what sounded like a voice among the four living creatures, saying, "Two pounds of wheat for a day's wages, and six pounds of barley for a day's wages, and do not damage the oil and the wine!"

The third horse speaks about a worldwide famine like never before. Remember in the time of Joseph in Egypt? God used Joseph to help with a worldwide famine crisis. Therefore, God must have put in a solution for His People at that time.

HELEN

He was the eldest son of Jacob and Rachel, right?

JODHI

Again, you are right. You must have paid attention in Sunday School. *(They both are laughing.)*

HELEN

They are the two people in the Bible that when they met, it was love at first sight. *(Helen is smiling.)*

JODHI

Yeah, almost like us.
(*Jodhi smiles and kisses Helen.*)

HELEN

So Jodhi tell me about the last horse? What does the 4th one
represents?

JODHI

(*Jodhi is reading. Revelation 6: 7-8*)

[7] *"When the Lamb opened the fourth seal, I heard the voice of the fourth living creature say, "Come!"* [8] *I looked, and there before me was a pale horse! Its rider was named Death, and Hades was following close behind him. They were given power over a fourth of the earth to kill by sword, famine and plague, and by the wild beasts of the earth."*

The fourth horse also speaks about the wars and the famine, but it includes plagues.

HELEN

What do you think that would be?

JODHI

That links into my last dream, I think.

HELEN

Tell me more about it.

JODHI

I saw the Anti-Christ again. It looked like a Middle East leader. Then I saw a dragon on the sea and a beast coming out of the sea. I also saw a beast coming out of the earth.

HELEN

Who is the dragon?

JODHI

The dragon represents the devil.

HELEN

And what about the Beast out of the sea?

JODHI

The Beast out of the sea represents a worldwide organisation who have the authority to make decrees and change law that will affect every country in the world. I saw the United Nations building.

Let me read you Chapter 13 in the Book of Revelation then you will get the picture clearer.

The Beast from the Sea

"The dragon stood on the sand of the sea. And I saw a beast rising up out of the sea, having seven heads and ten horns, and on his horns ten crowns, and on his heads a blasphemous name. [2] Now the beast which I saw was like a leopard, his feet were as the feet of a bear, and his mouth like the mouth of a lion. The dragon gave him his power, his throne, and great authority.

[3] And I saw one of his heads as if it had been mortally wounded, and his deadly wound was healed. And all the world marvelled and followed the beast. [4] So they worshipped the dragon who gave

authority to the beast; and they worshipped the beast, saying, "Who is like the beast? Who is able to make war with him?"

HELEN

Wow, it sounds like the movie "The Meg". A Megalodon shark that wants to attack the Saints.

JODHI

Yeah, you are right.

HELEN

You mentioned the beast coming out of the earth too.

JODHI

Yeah, I saw the beast coming out of the earth, and after that, I saw the Vatican and the Pope. It looked like they were trying to unite all religions under one.

Let me read you the rest of Chapter 13.

The Beast from the Earth

(Jodhi is reading. Revelation 13: 11-14)

"Then I saw another beast coming up out of the earth, and he had two horns like a lamb and spoke like a dragon. [12] And he exercises all the authority of the first beast in his presence, and causes the earth and those who dwell in it to worship the first beast, whose deadly wound was healed. [13] He performs great signs so that he even makes fire come down from heaven on the earth in the sight of men. [14] And he deceives those who dwell on the earth by those signs which he was granted to do in the sight of the beast, telling those who dwell on the earth to make an image to the beast who was wounded by the sword and lived."

HELEN

So, the 2 beasts will work together?

JODHI

That's correct. That's where the Mark of the Beast comes in.

HELEN

Explain more.

JODHI

(Jodhi is reading. Revelation 13: 15-18)

"He was granted the power to give breath to the image of the beast, that the image of the beast should both speak and cause as many as would not worship the image of the beast to be killed. [16] He causes all, both small and great, rich and poor, free and slave, to receive a mark on their right hand or on their foreheads, [17] and that no one may buy or sell except one who has the mark or the name of the beast, or the number of his name.[18] Here is wisdom. Let him who has understanding calculate the number of the beast, for it is the number of a man: His number is 666."

HELEN

What will be the Mark of the Beast?

JODHI

It will be a small microchip that will be injected into one's hand and one's forehead. The reason in one's hand is so that you can buy and sell without using a card or your phone or cash. You will simply just scan your hand over a sensor when you buy or sell.

HELEN

Why one's forehead also?

133

JODHI

On the forehead, they put in a chip that has all the data about you.
They can track you everywhere and can control your ways.
I think we are very close to this. When I was in Las Vegas, I saw a
programme on TV about people already start experimenting getting a
microchip. They are trying to promote it and make it sound good.
Then I dreamed that night about how they want everyone in the world
to have it. If you don't have it, you cannot buy or sell it.

HELEN

Wow, that's a lot for one day to think about.

JODHI

Yeah. I agree. Helen, I was thinking of tomorrow morning to visit an
old friend of mine on Staten Island. You are welcome to come with
me, or if you just want to chill out here, that's fine with me too.

HELEN

I think I will stay here and maybe see what shops they have around
here if you don't mind.

JODHI

That's fine with me. I won't be that long just catching up with him.

HELEN

No problem. Shall we go to bed? I am a bit tired.

JODHI

Yeah, let's go to bed.

(Jodhi is smiling.)
(They kiss each other and go to bed.)

Next Scene

(They wake up the next morning. Helen is cuddling Jodhi.)

HELEN

Morning sweetheart.

JODHI

Morning beautiful.

HELEN

Did you sleep well?

JODHI

Yeah, like a baby. And you?

HELEN

Yes, very well. I feel fresh like a daisy. So, you want to visit your friend today?

JODHI

Yeah, I need to phone him.

(Jodhi is ringing Ray. The phone is ringing. Ray is answering the phone.)

RAY

Hello.

JODHI

Hello old friend.

                              RAY

Is that you, Jodhi?

                              JODHI

Yeah, long time!

(Jodhi is laughing)

                              RAY

Wow, this is a surprise.

                              JODHI

Yeah. How are you doing?

                              RAY

Very good, my old friend and you?

                              JODHI

Very good, Ray.

                              RAY

Where are you now?

                              JODHI

I am right in your city.

                              RAY

Wow, you should come and see me.

JODHI

Yeah, I was thinking of coming and seeing you this morning if you are free.

RAY

That will be great. Long-time no see, brother!

JODHI

Ok, shall we meet at 11? We can try and solve all the problems of the world then. *Lol.*

RAY

Hahaha. That's perfect.

JODHI

Great. See you soon!

RAY

Cheers Jodhi.

JODHI

Cheers.

(Jodhi is hugging Helen. Jodhi phones the taxi.)

TAXI COMPANY

Good morning. Where do you want to go?

JODHI

I need a taxi from the Jane Hotel to 10 Broad Street, Staten Island.

TAXI COMPANY

No problem. When do you want the taxi for?

JODHI

For 10 am.

TAXI COMPANY

That's you booked. Our taxi driver Tony will be with you shortly.

(Jodhi goes for a shower and gets dressed. He gives Helen a hug.)

JODHI

Don't worry, I will be fine. I will give you a call once I reach Ray's house.

HELEN

Ok, take care. I will miss you.

(They kiss again.)

JODHI

I better go downstairs. The taxi would be here any minute now.

HELEN

Ok, sweetheart, bye.

JODHI

Bye-bye love.

(Jodhi goes downstairs to get a taxi. The taxi driver arrives. He is a young Italian guy.)

JODHI

Good morning. You must be Tony.

TAXI DRIVER

That's right, Sir. I am Tony Macaroni.

JODHI

Nice to meet you Tony.

TAXI DRIVER TONY

So why Staten Island today?

JODHI

I have an old friend called Ray that is living there that I haven't seen for a while.

(The sun is shining sharp in Jodhi's eyes. He is putting on his Ray-Ban glasses.)

TAXI DRIVER TONY

Ok, shall I turn some music on?

JODHI

Sure.

(The song starts playing "I love it" by Charli XCX.)

TAXI DRIVER TONY

I love this song!

(Tony is driving fast. They go over the Brooklyn bridge.)

JODHI

So, we are going to enter Bay Ridge soon?

TAXI DRIVER TONY

Yes, Saturday night fever area.

JODHI

So that's the Verrazano Bridge where they shot one of the scenes in the movie?

TAXI DRIVER TONY

Yeah, man. You are sharp.

(Tony turns up the music louder and starts driving faster. They start entering the Verrazano Bridge. Tony goes fast.)

JODHI

Watch out; the truck in front of us is not moving!!

TAXI DRIVER TONY

I will miss it! Don't worry!

(Tony makes a quick turn to the left. The car slips over to the other side and hits the bridge. Jodhi is unconscious. His left shoulder gets badly injured in the passenger door. Tony is also badly injured on his head, but he is still conscious. He phones 911.)

TAXI DRIVER TONY

Hi, could you please send out someone? We had a car crash on the Verrazano bridge, and both of us were badly injured.

911 EMERGENCY

We will send out someone immediately.

TONY

Thank you.

(Tony is looking at Jodhi. He feels Jodhi's pulse. His pulse is fine, but he is unconscious. Meanwhile, some other people stop at the scene to see if they are ok.)

WOMAN ON THE VERRAZANO BRIDGE

Are you ok? Can we help?

TONY

It's ok. I have already phoned 911. They will be here any moment. Thanks.

WOMAN ON THE VERRAZANO BRIDGE

Ok.

(An ambulance arrives at the scene. A paramedic called Jennifer comes to help.)

PARAMEDIC JENNIFER

Hi, my name is Jennifer. We need to get you out of here and into the Ambulance. Are you able to walk?

TONY

Yeah, but he will need help. He is unconscious. His name is Jodhi. I have checked his pulse. It's fine.

PARAMEDIC JENNIFER

Ok, let my colleague take you to the Ambulance. I will attend to him.

(Tony gets out of the car, and another assistant takes him to the Ambulance. Jennifer climbs over the seat to get to Jodhi. She pulls him slowly to the driving seat. She checks his pulse again. His pulse is fine. She asks her colleague to help her carry Jodhi to the Ambulance.

Both Jodhi and Tony are in the Ambulance with Jennifer. The Ambulance leaves the scene and drives to Mount Sinai Hospital in King's Highway Brooklyn.)

("Staying alive" song plays by the Bee Gees)

(They arrive at the Emergency Unit at Mount Sinai Hospital. They are taking Jodhi out of the ambulance on a stretcher and assisting Tony in walking. They get into the hospital and are taken to the emergency unit ward. Jennifer is looking at Jodhi's phone to look for personal contacts.)

PARAMEDIC JENNIFER

Tony, I saw a message on Jodhi's phone from a woman called Helen. Could that be his girlfriend?

TONY

I think so.

PARAMEDIC JENNIFER

Let me call her to let her know what has happened.

(Jennifer is calling Helen. The phone is ringing. Helen picks up.)

HELEN

Hello, Helen speaking.

PARAMEDIC JENNIFER

Hello Helen. It's Jennifer from Mount Sinai Hospital in Brooklyn. I am just phoning to let you know that Jodhi was in a car crash and he is with us now.

HELEN

Oh no, no!! Is he ok?

PARAMEDIC JENNIFER

He is alive but unconscious. If you can, come to the hospital.

HELEN

I will get a taxi immediately.

PARAMEDIC JENNIFER

It's Mount Sinai Hospital in Brooklyn. It's 3201 King's Highway. He is in the emergency ward.

HELEN

Ok. I hope Jodhi gets good care.

PARAMEDIC JENNIFER

We are doing our best. See you soon.

(Dr Green and Nurse Melody are coming into the emergency ward 10 to attend to Jodhi and Tony. Dr Green is first speaking with Tony.)

DR GREEN

Hello, I am Dr Green. How do you feel?

TONY

I am dizzy. Apart from that, I feel ok.

DR GREEN

Ok, we will first give you some painkillers then Nurse Melody will take care of the bruises on your head and face.

(Dr Green is looking at Jodhi. He monitors his heart rate. Also, he looks at his left arm.)

DR GREEN

Melody, could you also please take care of Mr Livingstone's left arm and take X-rays of his arm, please.

NURSE MELODY

I will do it, Dr Green.

DR GREEN

Also, keep an eye on him and let me know when he is conscious, please.

NURSE MELODY

Ok, Dr.

(Dr Green is leaving the ward. Melody attends to Tony. Helen arrives at the hospital. She rushes to reception at the Emergency Ward.)

GIRL AT RECEPTION

Good morning.

HELEN

Good morning. My boyfriend, Jodhi Livingstone, was taken in an hour ago.

GIRL AT RECEPTION

That's right. Dr Green has seen him, and staff nurse Melody is taking care of both of them. You are welcome to sit in the waiting room, and Melody will update you as things go on.

HELEN

Many thanks.

(Helen goes and sits in the waiting room. Jennifer, the Paramedic, comes to speak to Helen in the waiting room.)

PARAMEDIC JENNIFER

Good morning. I am Jennifer. I spoke earlier with you on the phone.

HELEN

Oh, nice to meet you, Jennifer.

PARAMEDIC JENNIFER

Same to you. I have Mr Livingstone's phone with me. I think someone has phoned him.

HELEN

Oh yeah, that must be his friend that he was going to visit. I will give him a call.

(Jennifer gives Jodhi's phone to Helen.)

PARAMEDIC JENNIFER

Jodhi is in good hands. Dr Green is our finest doctor.

HELEN

Thank you.

PARAMEDIC JENNIFER

Talk to you later.

HELEN

Ok, thanks.

(*Helen is phoning Ray. The phone is ringing. Ray is picking up the phone.*)

RAY

Hello, is that Jodhi?

HELEN

Hi Ray, it's Helen here. Jodhi's girlfriend.

RAY

Hi Helen. Is everything ok?

HELEN

Not really. Jodhi was in a car crash on his way to you. I love him so much that I can't afford to lose him. (*Tears go down Helen's cheek.*)

RAY

Gosh. Is he alive?

HELEN

Yeah, but they are taking care of him.

RAY

Ok, which hospital is he in?

HELEN

He is in Mount Sinai hospital on the King's Highway in the Emergency Ward.

RAY

Ok. Please let me know if there is anything I can do.

HELEN

It's ok Ray. The staff is really looking good after him.

RAY

I am glad. Please stay in contact.

HELEN

Will do Ray, bye for now.

RAY

Bye bye.

(Staff Nurse Melody arrives in the waiting room to see Helen. She talks to Helen.)

NURSE MELODY

Good morning, I am Melody.

HELEN

Morning, I am Helen.

NURSE MELODY

Pleased to meet you. Mr Livingstone is still unconscious. We have taken X-rays, and we are just waiting for Dr Green to give us a diagnosis and prognosis.

HELEN

Thank you, Melody.

NURSE MELODY

In the meantime, we can just pray that Jesus will awake Mr Livingstone out of his unconscious state.

148

HELEN

Yeah, that's right. It sounds like you are also a Christian.

NURSE MELODY

Yeah, I am. Do you want me to pray with you?

HELEN

That will be great if you can.

NURSE MELODY

Ok, that's my pleasure.

(Nurse Melody is sitting next to Helen and holding Helen's hand. She starts praying for Jodhi.)

NURSE MELODY

Father, we pray in Jesus's name that you can fully awake Mr Livingstone to his full consciousness. We also pray that He will have an encounter with your Son Jesus and that he be healed completely. Amen.

HELEN

Amen. That was a lovely prayer. Thank you so much Melody.

(Helen is waiting in the waiting room.)

(The song plays "I love Angels instead " by Robbie Williams.)

(Dr Green is coming to see Helen.)

DR GREEN

Hello. I am Dr Green. You must be Mr Livingstone's friend or, shall I say, girlfriend.

(Dr Green is smiling.)

HELEN

Yes, Doctor.

(Helen is blushing.)

DR GREEN

Well, I have some good news for you. Mr Livingstone is awake.

HELEN

Thank God. That's very good news.

DR GREEN

Indeed, but I have also looked at his left arm. We need to do a small operation.

HELEN

Is it serious?

DR GREEN

He will be fine. His left shoulder joint is fractured because of the high impact of the accident. Also, his left arm triceps are seriously damaged, and the shoulder bone is fractured.
The nerves throughout his left arm got injured. So, what we will do is get our Surgeon, Dr Struwig, who will do an operation on his left arm.

Our Anaesthetist Jonell Victor will be here soon. He will be released from the hospital in 3 days' time. So, it's maybe a good time if you go and see him now before we get him anaesthetized. After he is released from the hospital, he would need to go for physiotherapy in 2 weeks' time.

HELEN

Ok, thank you, Doctor.

(Dr Green is taking Helen to see Jodhi. They enter the ward and go to his bed. Helen is crying and very happy to see Jodhi.)

DR GREEN

Here is your lovely Helen.

JODHI

(Jodhi is smiling.)

Hello, Helen from Heaven.

HELEN

I am so happy to see you. Thank God you are alive. Staff Nurse Melody and I have been praying for you. See God answers prayer!

(Helen gives Jodhi a kiss.)

JODHI

Indeed, He does.

HELEN

How are you feeling?

JODHI

I am feeling good, Helen. My arm is very sore, but that will get fixed. Praise God!

(Jodhi is smiling.)

HELEN

Dr Green told me you are going to be in hospital for 2 nights after your surgery. I will pray for you.

JODHI

Thank you, Helen, that means the world to me.

HELEN

You are welcome, my love.
(They kiss each other.)

(Surgeon Dr Struwig and Anaesthetist Jonell Victor are entering the ward to see Jodhi.)

DR STRUWIG

Good evening you two. We are going to prepare now for the Surgery. Miss Taylor if you could say goodbye to Mr Livingstone.
(Helen gives Jodhi a hug.)

HELEN

Goodbye Jodhi.

JODHI

Bye Helen. I will see you soon.

(Jodhi is smiling.)

(Helen is leaving the ward.)

DR STRUWIG

Mr Livingstone, this is our Anaesthetist, Jonell Victor. She is going to give you an anaesthetic and morphine. You will be out for a few hours while I will perform the surgery.

JODHI

Ok, doctor.

(Anaesthetist Jonell Victor is attending to Jodhi.)

ANAESTHESIST JONELL VICTOR

Good evening Mr Livingstone. Is this the first time you are getting anaesthesia?

JODHI

Yes, Doctor, never before.

ANAESTHESIST JONELL VICTOR

Well, nothing to worry about. It will be all good. I am going to give you an anaesthetic now and morphine after the operation. You will start feeling sleepy, you will lose consciousness, and after a few hours, regain consciousness back.

JODHI

I understand, Doctor.

Next Scene

(Anaesthetist Jonell Victor gives Jodhi an anaesthetic. He starts to lose consciousness. He sees is a Bright Light. The next moment Jesus appears to Him as the Resurrected Christ. In Jesus hands one can still see the marks of the nails although it's healed)

JESUS

Jodhi, I have come to speak about your mission on earth. You have been called together with Helen to fulfil a great mission for me on earth. I have given you 4 dreams to prepare you for your mission.
I will give Helen a dream as well - to confirm and reassure her that I have called both of you together. I will give you more understanding about the 4 dreams, but I want you and Helen to go to Rome.
At the fountain of the "The Fontana Della Barcaccia" in Rome, I will give you more revelation about what to do. I am with you and Helen, so do not fear.

(Jesus disappears.)

(Helen is taking a taxi to the Jane Hotel. She is going to bed. She has a dream. She sees Jodhi and her holding hands together on a beach in Cape Town. They are married. She awakes and ponders about it.)

(It's the next day, and Jodhi is awake. The nurse Melody is talking with him.)

NURSE MELODY

Morning Mr Livingstone. How do you feel?

JODHI

Morning. I feel ok. My arm is a bit sore.

NURSE MELODY

Yeah, that will take a while, but the wound will heal with time. God heal wounds in time.

JODHI

Well, you must be a believer then.

NURSE MELODY

Yes, I am. I prayed with Helen for you.

JODHI

I can assure you that God has listened to you. I had a visitation by Jesus while the surgery was performed. I will tell you a bit later before I get out of the hospital.

NURSE MELODY

Wow! That's very exciting news Mr Livingstone.

(It's the third day, and the operating team is saying goodbye to Jodhi. Helen is also there.)

DR STRUWIG

Good day Mr Livingstone.

JODHI

Good morning Dr Struwig.

DR STRUWIG

Well, I am happy to say that your surgery was successful.

156

JODHI

Thanks Dr Struwig.

DR GREEN

I know you are going to heal quickly. I wish you all the best for the future.

JODHI

Thank you, Dr Green, for taking care of me. You are so kind. I feel much better.

(The song "The Victor" by Keith Green plays in the background.)

ANAESTHESIST JONELL VICTOR

All the best to you, Mr Livingstone. Helen is in the waiting room. Staff nurse Melody will take you to her.

JODHI

Thank you very much. I don't have the words to thank you, but I thank you.

ANAESTHESIST JONELL VICTOR

You are most welcome, Mr Livingstone. We are all a team here working together.

JODHI

That's true. Teamwork makes the dream work. (*Jodhi is smiling.*) How is the taxi driver doing?

ANAESTHESIST JONELL VICTOR

He is fine. He was released the next day after the accident.

JODHI

That's good news.

(Nurse Melody is taking Jodhi to Helen.)

158

That's good news.

(Nurse Melody is taking Jodhi to Helen.)

Next Scene

(Jodhi meets Helen. They kiss and take a taxi to the Jane Hotel. They arrive at the Jane Hotel. Jodhi tells Helen about his divine experience in hospital with the Resurrected Lord and why He commanded him to go to Rome.)

JODHI

I have missed you the last few days. You are my love.

HELEN

Me too, honey! *(Jodhi and Helen kiss.)*

JODHI

You know, such a lot of things have happened in the hospital. I have come out as a new man. Completely changed with a clear vision.

HELEN

What do you mean?

JODHI

I mean, I had an encounter with the Risen Lord.

HELEN

What?

(Helen is in awe.)

JODHI

Yeah, He told me that He gave me the 4 dreams and that He wants me to go to Rome and give me more revelation.

159

HELEN

That's amazing.

JODHI

Yeah. Will you go with me?

HELEN

Yes of course, but I think we need to make a few phone calls first.

JODHI

Yes, you are right. I will phone my kids, and you can phone your parents. It's time to go on a real mission.

HELEN

Yeah, you are right. Don't forget to phone Mr Mcdonald that offered you the job.

JODHI

Yeah, how could I forget?

HELEN

Let's do it now.

(Jodhi and Helen are making phone calls. They book a taxi for the airport.
They go outside, and the taxi is waiting for them outside the hotel.)

(The scene stops where the movie has started with the Taxi driver Rich picking up Jodhi and Helen.)

(Helen and Jodhi arrive in Rome. They are at "The Fontana Della Barcaccia".)

(They are looking at the Fountain. Jodhi goes into a trance and sees Jesus speaking to him.)

JESUS

Jodhi, you are My well-beloved servant. Thanks for your obedience. I always reward obedience. I have brought you here so that I can tell you what you must do. I have chosen Southern Africa as my place of safety for My children. Read the passage of Zephaniah 3:10-17 with Revelation 7 and 14 later with Helen. You will meet a Chinese woman called Ann standing at the Spanish Steps buying Jasmine flowers. I have chosen her as a vessel to work with you and Helen.

She will help you set up a new digital currency for My beloved people. It will be a currency for My chosen people to buy and sell goods in the time of the Great Tribulation. I have chosen Cape Town for the end time. It's not called by accident the Cape of Good Hope. It will be a place of safety for my children.

You should open a Bank for Christians in Cape Town, South Africa. I want you and Helen to go to Cape Town and take Ann with you. Before that I want you and Helen to go to Turin. My shroud is on public display this week there. When you are there, I will reveal more to you.

(Jesus disappears.)

(Jodhi and Helen are walking towards the Spanish Steps. A flower girl is selling Jasmine flowers. A Chinese woman is buying some Jasmine flowers. Jodhi also goes to buy Jasmine flowers for Helen. He starts speaking with the Chinese woman.)

JODHI

Hi, you must be Ann.

(Ann is in awe)

ANN

How do you know my name?

JODHI

I have this strange gift of hearing a voice. Not what women wants but what God wants.

(Jodhi and Helen are laughing.)

ANN

You must be a Psychic.

JODHI

Let's say I can spot someone important.

ANN

Thanks for the compliment.

JODHI

You are very welcome. Let me introduce you. This is Helen.

HELEN

Nice to meet you, Ann.

(Helen and Ann shake hands.)

JODHI

I am Jodhi.

(*Jodhi and Ann shake hands.*)

JODHI

Are you from Rome?

ANN

Yes, I only moved here recently. My father is Italian, and my mother is from Shanghai, China.

JODHI

That's interesting. Are you on your own or with someone?

ANN

On my own.

JODHI

Well, you are welcome to join us for a cup of coffee if you want.

ANN

That will be great. Always nice to meet new friends.

JODHI

I have heard there is a good coffee shop around the corner of the Pantheon called "Sant' Eustachio II Caffe".

ANN

Yeah, I know the coffee shop. It would be lovely to join you.

HELEN

Great, I am excited! I also want to see the Pantheon.

JODHI

Ok, let me stop a taxi.

Next Scene

(*Jodhi stops a taxi and they all get into the taxi and drive to the coffee shop.*)

JODHI

Hi. Can you take us to Sant' Eustachio II Caffe?

TAXI DRIVER

Yes, sure, Sir.

JODHI

Thanks. What's your good name?

TAXI DRIVER

I am Steven, Sir.

JODHI

Nice to meet you, Steven. Are you from here?

TAXI DRIVER STEVEN

I live here now because my father's family is from here, but I grew up in Scotland. My mother is Scottish.

JODHI

Oh, great, we have something in common. I am also half Scottish. My name is Jodhi.

TAXI DRIVER STEVEN

That's great, but you sound American.

JODHI

I spent most of my life in the US.

TAXI DRIVER STEVEN

That explains it. So, are all 3 of you travelling together?

JODHI

We have just met Ann today, so we are all going for a coffee.

TAXI DRIVER STEVEN

Wow, that's fantastic. They say all roads leads to Rome. It seems your paths have been destined.

JODHI

You have no idea.

TAXI DRIVER STEVEN

Right guys, we are here.

JODHI

Thank you so much, Steven. I wish you God's speed.

TAXI DRIVER STEVEN

Same to you. Bye.

Next Scene

(They all wave at Steven. They go to the Sant' Eustachio II Caffe. They sit at a table outside, and a waitress Dora serves them.)

WAITRESS DORA

Good morning! I am Dora, your waitress for this morning.

JODHI

Good morning Dora! Nice to meet you.

WAITRESS DORA

Here is the menu for you. We have a variety of coffee beans from all over the world.

JODHI

Yeah, I have heard. You have the best coffee in town.

(Jodhi is smiling.)

WAITRESS DORA

That's correct. I will be back soon to take your order.

JODHI

Thanks.

(They are all looking at the menu. The girls choose the Ethiopian Arabic beans and Jodhi choose expresso.}

(Dora is coming to take their order.)

WAITRESS DORA

It looks like you are ready.

JODHI

Yes, the girls want Ethiopian Arabic beans.

WAITRESS DORA

Great, and for you?

JODHI

While in Rome I will go for an Italian Expresso.

WAITRESS DORA

Great!

(Dora walks back into the café to place the order.)

JODHI

So, Ann, are you a student or are you working?

ANN

Well, I studied investment banking in Japan for a couple of years while doing some trading on Bitcoin on the quiet.

JODHI

That's very interesting. Can you tell me more about Bitcoin? As far as I know, that was the first cryptocurrency that started, and it all happened in Japan.

ANN

Yeah, the person that started it is still unknown. All I know is that I made good money with it.

JODHI

Can you tell us more about how crypto works? If we would, for instance, want to start our own cryptocurrency.

ANN

Well, that's a good idea. There are many out there today.

JODHI

Will you be able to help us with that?

ANN

Yeah, sure, I also like new challenges.

JODHI

We are actually heading out to Cape Town, South Africa, to open a new online digital bank with a new cryptocurrency.

HELEN

Are we?

(*Helen is taken by surprise.*)

JODHI

Sorry, Helen, I still meant to tell you about that, but men get forgetful.

(*smiles apologetically*)

HELEN

That's ok. I will still love you tomorrow. Anything else I should know?

(Helen is smiling)

JODHI

Actually yes, we are going to Milan and Turin for 2 days.

HELEN

Oh nice! I am sure that is going to be good!!

JODHI

For sure. Well, after that we would go to Cape Town. I know this sounds impulsive, but Ann, you are welcome to join us. You seem like the right girl to join our team.

ANN

You know what? I have learned that the best things happen spontaneously. The things that you never plan turn out to be the special things in life.

JODHI

I couldn't agree more. What can I say – we have met our match. Everything in our lives happens spontaneously. Helen and I have only known each other for 2 weeks now.

ANN

Well, I will join the joy ride. I just need to let my parents know. They were asking me the other day what my plans for the future are. I couldn't answer them, but now I can. *(Ann is smiling.)*

(The song plays "Join the Joyride" by Roxette.)

JODHI

So, when we back in Rome we can meet you at the airport. I hope it's
not too short notice for you.

ANN

No, I am a free spirit. It sounds like a good plan to me.

*(Dora brings the order. They are having a nice time together. Jodhi
and Helen takes a taxi to their hotel, and they pass the Vatican.)*

(Jodhi and Helen are in Milan. They are looking at the bronze horse statue of Leonardo Da Vinci.)

JODHI

You know what, Helen; this statue was actually 500 years in the making.

HELEN

How come?

JODHI

Leonardo Da Vinci was challenged by Ludovico, the Duke of Milan, to build the largest equestrian statue the world had ever seen in honour of his father, Francesco.
In 1493 he presented a 24-foot clay model on the occasion of Ludovico's daughter's wedding, from which a bronze horse could be made.

During the Italian wars, when the French troops turned on Ludicovo, he was forced to use 80 tons of bronze that had been set aside for the horse to make weapons for the battle of Fornova, the first of many battles in the Italian Wars, which enveloped Northern Italy.

HELEN

What happened then with the horse?

JODHI

Then in 1499, invading French archers used the huge horse statue for target practice, reducing the fragile model to ruins and marking the end of the artistic boom times. To make it even worse, Da Vinci's moulds and sketches of the original horse were lost, and the project was abandoned.

HELEN

You are a genius with your history!

JODHI

Yeah, I was a straight-A student in history in my time.

(*Jodhi smiles*)

HELEN

So, the horse statue was never completed in his time?

JODHI

No, never. It was only five centuries later that Leonardo Da Vinci's "lost notebooks" were found in the Biblioteca Nationale in Madrid in 1965, including his sketches for the horse. In Allentown, Pennsylvania, a retired pilot and collector of Renaissance art Charles Dent read about the notebooks and the story of the never-built horse in the National Geographic in 1977 and decided to complete the story. He brought on the sculpture Nina Akamu to realize the design from Da Vinci's original drawings. Unfortunately, Charles Dent died in 1994 before he could see his project completed.

HELEN

So sad.

JODHI

Yeah, it is sad but true. This final bronze horse was installed in Milan in 1999, 500 years after the original model was destroyed.

HELEN

Amazing, I bet you not a lot of people know the history behind this horse statue.

JODHI

Yeah, it's a fascinating story. A story of stories. Let's go to Turin before we fly back to Rome.

HELEN

Sure love.

Next Scene

(Jodhi and Helen are in Turin looking at the shroud of Jesus on public display. Jesus appears to Jodhi while he is looking at the shroud.)

JESUS

Jodhi, as you see My shroud, you can see the marks of My wounds. I was wounded by the nails in My wrists and also the Crown of thorns on My head. The evil one is trying to copy it by giving a microchip on the forehands and on the foreheads of people.
This is the Mark of the Beast to control people and also not allow them to buy or sell without it. The number of the Mark of the Beast is 666.

I am going to mark My chosen people with My name. That is the Seal of God in the Book of Revelation. It's for My chosen people to buy and sell. I want you to create a wristband. It will be a wristband for Christians with the symbol 888. The numerical values of the name "Jesus" in the Greek Alphabet sum up to 888.

Lastly, when you are in Cape Town, I want you to set up an Airline for My Saints, which you must call Saints 888 Airline. When you are in Cape Town, meet up with your friend Ernst. He will help you to set up this Airline. I will reveal more to you when you are there. I am with you wherever you go.

(Jesus disappears.)

(Jodhi and Helen are taking a flight back to Rome. They meet Ann at the airport. They all fly together to Cape Town. They arrive in Cape town and get a taxi to the One and Only hotel on the Waterfront.)

(Jodhi Helen and Ann are sitting in a restaurant in the One and Only hotel having drinks.)

JODHI

I have a very good friend here in Cape Town. He was with me in primary school. He is into the Airline business. He will help us set up an Airline business for God's Saints.

Let me give him a call to meet us.

HELEN

Airline business?? My word Jodhi, are we taking over the world?! *(Helen smiles in amazement.)*

JODHI

I think God is. *(Jodhi smiles)*

(Jodhi is calling his friend Ernst. The phone rings. Ernst is picking up the phone.)

ERNST

That's a surprise. How are you doing, my good friend?

JODHI

I am doing very well, Ernst. Guess what?

ERNST

Tell me.

JODHI

I am very close to you right now.

ERNST

You are joking! Are you in South Africa?

JODHI

Yes, brother. I am in the One and Only at the Waterfront.

ERNST

My word! That's brilliant news!

JODHI

Yes, I was wondering if you have time to meet us this afternoon?

ERNST

Of course. What time?

JODHI

Anytime. We are sitting now in the restaurant in the One and Only, having a few drinks. You can join us if you want.

ERNST

Ok, that's Ace. I will let Emma drive me back. I need to have a few drinks with my good old friend. We will see you soon.

JODHI

That will be brilliant. Looking forward.

ERNST

See you soon.

JODHI

Great Ernst.

(Ernst and Emma arrive at the One and Only hotel. They walk into the restaurant and meet Jodhi, Helen and Ann.)

ERNST

Wow, what a fantastic surprise.

JODHI

Yeah, it's good to see you, Ernst.

ERNST

Yes, so many things have happened since I saw you last. You know, I met Emma on a business trip to London. We got married last year, and she is expecting our first child.

JODHI

I am so happy for you both. Do you know if it's a girl or a boy?

ERNST

Yes, it's a girl. We are going to call her Mulan.

JODHI

Oh, after the Disney character. That's a brave girl.

HELEN

Congratulations, beautiful Emma. I am very happy for you.

ANN

Yeah, me too.

EMMA

Thank you very much.

ERNST

So how come you are in Cape Town?

JODHI

Well, that is what I want to discuss with you.

ERNST

I am all ears.

JODHI

We are busy setting up a new digital online bank in Cape Town with Ann, and we want to start a new Airline business.

ERNST

Wow, you are thinking mega big. I like that.

(*Ernst is laughing.*)

JODHI

Yeah, I will tell you the story later about what led up to that, but we wanted to know if you want to join us in the project?

ERNST

You know me. I am always up for something new and challenging.
I think Emma can play a big part in this. She has family in Shanghai
that's into building airbuses and I have been in the airline business
most of my life as you know.

JODHI

Yes. That's amazing. Ann is also originally from Shanghai.

EMMA

Wow, what a small world! I will be pleased to be part of this project.

JODHI

I know. We have a great team. Let's do it.

(They enjoy a few drinks together. Ernst and Emma say goodbye.)

Scene at Physio at Durbanville Medic Clinic

JODHI

Good morning. I am here for my appointment.

RECEPTIONIST PAMELA

Good morning. Are you Mr Livingstone?

JODHI

That's correct.

RECEPTIO\IST PAMELA

You can go through; Molly, our Physiotherapist, is waiting for you.
(Jodhi goes to meet the physiotherapist Molly.)

MOLLY

Good morning Mr Livingstone.

JODHI

Good morning.

MOLLY

I see you are from the USA?

JODHI

Yes, I am, but originally, I come from here.

MOLLY

I can hear you haven't lost your accent.

JODHI

Yes, I am too much of a South African in my heart to lose my accent.

MOLLY

That's good. Never lose your identity. God has great plans for this country.

JODHI

I agree. You can tell South Africa this is my song.

MOLLY

So, I heard , Mr Livingstone, you had a bad injury on your left arm.

JODHI

Yes, I am just happy to survive the crash. Jesus is great!

MOLLY

I see you are a passionate Christian. Just like David Livingstone, who came to Africa.

JODHI

Yes, I like his story. I take inspiration from it. You know, right at the beginning of his missionary work in Africa, he got attacked by a Lion while trying to save a woman. He injured his left arm and would let nothing stand in his way of fulfilling his ministry.

MOLLY

Well, yes, he was a brave man. So, let's see what we can do on your arm.

(Molly is giving him some exercises to do.)

MOLLY

I think your arm will heal up without a problem.

JODHI

Thank you very much, Molly. You have the heart of Molly in Titanic. She wanted to save as many passengers as possible in the crises.

MOLLY

Thank you very much. I liked that movie a lot. I am fortunate to be in this profession to help many people in their recovery.

JODHI

Yes, everyone of God's children has been given a part to play in His Masterplan.

(Jodhi leaves the physio. He heads back to the hotel to phone his kids, Christian and Jessica, and to speak to his ex-wife Emily to arrange for the kids to come to Cape Town for a holiday.)

Next Scene

Jodhi's kids arrive at the Airport in Cape Town

(Christian and Jessica come through the Gates at the airport. Jessica runs to Jodhi, and Christian is very excited. Jodhi hugs them and introduces Helen to them. Tears fall.)

(They take a taxi to the hotel. They are sitting in the lounge at the hotel and catching up on everything that has happened since he left the house.)

JODHI

So, you guys are happy to be in Cape Town?

JESSICA

Umm yeah, I really like it!

CHRISTIAN

It's nice.

JODHI

Is this what you were expecting?

CHRISTIAN

More than what I expected.

JODHI

Well, tomorrow I am going to take you to Paarl Rock. You are going to love it.

JESSICA

What is Paarl Rock?

JODHI

It's a big rock in Paarl, an hour's drive from here, and you can see it from afar.

JESSICA

Does it look like the Rock in Lion King, because that Rock you could also see from afar off?

JODHI

You are right, Jessica; it's almost like Pride Rock. They have a monument there dedicated to the Afrikaans language. It's the youngest language in the world.

CHRISTIAN

Wow, I am glad you taught me some Afrikaans.

JODHI

It's important. It's part of our heritage.

JESSICA

You started teaching me too. I want to learn more.

JODHI

No worries, Jessica, I will teach you a lot more. Let's go to sleep. You guys had a long flight, and we have to be up early tomorrow morning.

Scene at Paarl Rock

(Jodhi, Helen, Christian and Jessica are walking around the Afrikaans Language Monument and stop at a place of writing on the stones.)

JODHI

It's part of our heart and soul. You see this inscription? "Dit is ons erns. "

CHRISTIAN

What does it mean?

JODHI

It means "We are serious about this". It dates back to 1905 when politician JH Hofmeyer held a speech on language rights entitled "Is't u Ernst?"

JESSICA

Why are they serious about this?

JODHI

It resembles our heritage of how many nations came together and formed a common language.

HELEN

Yes, it's like the English language is most spoken over the world, but Afrikaans is formed uniquely from different languages from European countries.

JODHI

You are learning, Helen.

(*They all laugh.*)

HELEN

Shall we drive back? I think the children would love to swim in the sea.

CHRISTIAN

Yeah, I can't wait.

JESSICA

That would be so nice. Christian and I love swimming.

JODHI

So, let's go.

(They drive back to the hotel. Back at the hotel, Jodhi is speaking with his children. He tells them that he is going to propose to Helen the next day. They are very happy.)

Scene at the hotel where Jodhi is speaking to his children in private

JODHI

Well, kids, I have something to tell you.

JESSICA

What is that?

JODHI

How do you feel about Helen?

JESSICA

I think she is so nice. I want to cuddle her.

CHRISTIAN

Yeah, she seems lovely. I can see why you love her.

JODHI

Well, I am going to propose to her tomorrow.

JESSICA

Yippee! That will be wonderful.

CHRISTIAN

I am so happy for you.

(They all 3 have a family hug.)

Scene at the 12 Apostles Hotel on Table Mountain. Jodhi is proposing to Helen.

(The song plays of Kurt Darren, "It's heaven on Table Mountain.")

(Jodhi and Helen are alone at the 12 Apostles hotel. They are having a nice dinner together in the restaurant. They go out for a walk at the Rock Garden and then go to the big garden where weddings take place.

It has a very nice sea view. Helen thanks Jodhi for the night, but he has one more surprise. They hold hands.

HELEN

Well, Mr handsome, thank you for such a lovely evening. You've wined me, you've dined me, you swept me off my feet. I couldn't ask for more.

JODHI

Thank you, Miss beautiful. I have one more thing planned, but we need to go to the ballroom.

HELEN

You are full of surprises, like always.

JODHI

Let's go.

(Jodhi takes Helen's hand and walks with her towards the empty ballroom. There is a piano.)

JODHI

I know you are good at playing the piano. Could you please play me this song while I want to read something to you?

HELEN

Sure honey.

(Helen is sitting in front of the piano, and Jodhi is standing. He takes 2 papers out of his pocket.

*One paper has the song **'Holy and Anointed One'** with lyrics, chords and some wording " Your name is like honey on my lips ". The other One has extracts of the book of Songs of Solomon in the Bible. He gives her the one with the song, and he keeps the one with the extracts of the Book of Song of Solomon. Helen starts playing the song on the piano, and Jodhi reads extracts of the book of Song of Solomon to her.)*

Like a lily among thorns,
So is my darling among the maidens.

My dove in the clefts of the rock,
In the hiding places on the mountainside,
show me your face,
let me hear your voice;
for your voice is sweet,
and your face is lovely.

How beautiful you are, my darling!
Oh how beautiful!
The vines are in blossom;
They give forth fragrance.
Arise, my love, my beautiful one,
and come away."

HELEN

That's so beautiful!! I am your Lily of the Valley.

JODHI

And I am yours.

(They kiss.)

JODHI

You know I love you very much. I can see heaven in your blue eyes.

HELEN

(Helen is blushing.)

I do, and you know I love you too.

JODHI

You made my heart whole again, but there is one more thing to do.

HELEN

What is that?

*(Jodhi goes on his knees and takes out a diamond ring and proposes
to her.)*

JODHI

Will you marry me?

HELEN

Of course.

*(She jumps up and kisses him. He puts the ring on her finger, and the song **"Diamonds" of Rihanna plays**. They walk to the outside terrace overlooking the sea. They order champagne and make a toast.)*

JODHI

May our future shine bright together like this diamond.

HELEN

Ditto.

BLOUBERG WEDDING SCENE

(They are in the Church at Bloubergstrand. The Church Pastor, Kobus Genis, has just married them, and he is presenting them to the guests.)

PASTOR KOBUS

I present you, Mr and Mrs Livingstone.

*(They are all cheering while Jodhi is giving Helen a kiss. The song plays **"Oceans (Where Feet May Fail)" – Hillsong United***

(They walk out of the church as the people throw confetti on them. Mr McDonald is also there and congratulates the couple and gives them a wedding horseshoe gift.)

MR MCDONALD

Well, Jodhi, congratulations. I see things have turned out bright for you in a very swift way.

JODHI

What can I say? God is good.

MR MCDONALD

Well, I have a gift for both of you.

(Mr Mcdonald takes a wedding horseshoe out of a bag and gives it to them.)

May this wedding horseshoe bring good luck, and may God bless you with beautiful children.

HELEN

That's so beautiful. Thank you so much, Mr Mcdonald.

MR MCDONALD

You are welcome! You have found a beloved man, and he has found the perfect flower in you!

JODHI

Thank you, Mr Mcdonald. I will look well after her.

MR MCDONALD

I am sure you will.

Scene at Blue Peter Hotel Bloubergstrand

(They are at the Wedding reception. The place is full of white Lilies. They have the opening dance.)

(Blake Sheldon and Gwen Stefani's song "Nobody but you" plays.)

JODHI

May I say... You look amazing today, my Love.
Oh, you have touched my heart from the very first day that I saw you.
And you continue to do so every single day since...

HELEN

May I say, Mr Handsome, Ditto again.

(*They are smiling.*)

(*At the end of the night, everyone has left. They are walking barefoot with wedding clothes on the beach into the water at Bloubergstrand.*)

The song plays "Heaven is a place on earth" by Belinda Carlisle.

THE END

SONG LIST:

1) "Who let the dogs out" by Baha Men
2) "Whenever, wherever" by Shakira
3) "Get Ready" by Blake & Pitbull
4) "Mr Brightside" Destiny is calling by The Killers
5) "Viva Las Vegas" by Elvis Presley
6) "Money Towers" by Lydmor.
7) "Toxic" by Britney Spears
8) "I Want Candy" by Charli XCX
9) "24K Magic" by Bruno Mars
10) " It's a beautiful day" by U2
11) "Genesis" by Dua Lipa
12) "I should be so Lucky" by Kylie Minogue
13) "Tonight is going to be a good night" by The Black-Eyed Peas.
14) "Bring the Old Town" by Lil Nas X & Billy Ray Cyrus
15) "She drives me crazy" by Fine Young Cannibals
16) "Take me anywhere" by Rita Ora
17) "New York New York" by Frank Sinatra
18) "Stock Market Rap" by Smart Songs
19) " International Love" by Pitbull.
20) "I love it" by Charli XCX
21) " Staying alive" song plays by the Bee Gees.
22) "I love Angels instead" by Robbie Williams
23) "The Victor" by Keith Green
24) "Join the Joyride" by Roxette
25) "It's heaven on Table mountain" by Kurt Darren
26) "Diamonds" by Rihanna
27) "Oceans (Where Feet May Fail)" Hillsong United
28) "Nobody but you "Blake Sheldon and Gwen Stefani
29) "Heaven is a place on earth "by Belinda Carlisle

9 781915 942142